# OUR FOREVER HOME

Author: Ronald S. Javor

Illustrator: Sandra J. Hoover

Design Editor: Laraine Hutcherson

Our Forever Home



ISBN: 9798565640953

Library of Congress Control Number: 2020925702

Manufactured in the United States of America.

www.ronaldjavorbooks.com

At least 50% of all profits from this book will be donated to organizations assisting homeless and lower income households.

Ronald Javor writes books for younger readers to help them learn about important social issues and to question misleading stereotypes. His work includes seven children's books about children facing and overcoming challenges and barriers such as homelessness and disabilities.

More information about him and these books may be found at his website, ronaldjavorbooks.com, and on Amazon.

Other children's books he has written include:

"Homer Finds a Home"
"Wendy's Wonderful Window"
"Jerome Builds a New Home"
"Many Houses, Many Homes"
"Sam and Sue's Space Adventure"
"Cayla's Special Dark Glasses"
"Bailey's Path"

"Never doubt that a small group of thoughtful,
committed citizens can change the world;
indeed, it's the only thing that ever has."

*Margaret Mead, Cultural Anthropologist*
*Inaugurating the first Earth Day, April 22, 1970.*

**Fifty Years Later…**

"To put it simply, the state of the planet is broken…Humanity is waging a war on nature…Let's be clear: human activities are at the root of our descent towards chaos…

"But that means human action can help solve it…Now is the time to transform humankind's relationship with the natural world – and with each other.

"And we must do so together…Solidarity is humanity. Solidarity is survival."

*United Nations Secretary-General Antonio Guterres*
*United Nations Climate Summit, December 2, 2020*

This book is dedicated to all those people,
both young and old, and private and government
organizations who are trying to make large or small
differences to stop the increasing momentum
of climate change, habitat destruction,
unnecessary hunting, profiteering from living things,
and, ultimately, animal suffering and extinctions.

# ACKNOWLEDGEMENTS

A note to the reader. This book was written for you! I hope you enjoy it and that you will take the advice of Dodo and Lonesome George and do your part to join with others to combat climate change, glŏbal warming, and extinctions.

Special thanks have been earned by many. First, a big shout-out to Sandra Hoover and Laraine Hutcherson, the illustrator and design editor who stuck with me through many drafts so that you would be able to read this. In defense of them, any factual or typographical errors you may find are mine alone.

Inspiration and support came from many people. Along with others who provided encouragement, these included, but definitely aren't limited to, Tom DiFiore, an animal lover who encouraged the evolution from a short story to this full-length book; Mr. Mel Webster, my junior high school science teacher who decades ago triggered my imagination and interest in prehistoric animals and fossils; and my Mother who schlepped us on weekends in an old station wagon to remote sites for "fossil-digging adventures."

Finally, a special posthumous (after death) thank you to Lonesome George whom I met at the Galapagos Conservancy Center in 2008 and whose plight remained a beacon for me.

# Table of Contents

# CHAPTER 1

## *A STRANGE GATE APPEARS*

**THE LONG, DUSTY, WINDING PATH** came to a sudden end in front of an odd-looking towering dark gate in the middle of nowhere. The gate was constructed of a smooth glistening metallic material. It stood about ten feet tall and the dirt walkway ended directly in front of it. Large green trees and bushes sprouted on either side of it, and a bright blue sky shined above it. Its top brace had the words, "OUR FOREVER HOME" written in large gold letters on a black background.

No other clue was apparent to identify what the gate was or why it was there. A smaller old sign stood on the ground in front of one of the two gate posts that said, in large black capital letters, "Condors Not Welcome." The other gate post had a similar sign in front of it, but it was brand new and its black letters read, "Welcome Home, Lonesome George!"

The space and air between the gateposts seemed to shimmer, looking like a steamy mirage rising off hot pavement on a sweltering day. Someone standing outside on the path only could see a vast area of open space through the gate, with bright greens, browns, blues, and many of the other varied colors that flowers produce all blurred by the gate's iridescent opening.

OUR FOREVER HOME
HOME

Those colors formed a variety of unclear shapes that seemed to be small and large trees of all kinds and low rolling hills sweeping up to towering mountains. The sky inside also was blue, but a different, brighter blue and with fewer clouds than the sky outside the gate. It seemed to be a peaceful serene landscape without any buildings, bridges, roads, or any other man-made structures anywhere in sight.

A single small bee slowly buzzed and fluttered in circles outside the large gate. After a few moments, it turned and flew towards the shimmering opening. At the last second before entering between the gateposts, the bee suddenly swerved away and soared over the gate, flying quickly away.

Soon after that happened, a tiny brown field mouse carefully crept on the ground towards the gate, its nose quivering and its tail held straight up and taut as it warily investigated the unusual sight. It slowly stepped forward until it was within inches of the iridescent opening. Then it suddenly squeaked loudly, jumped away, and scampered into the nearby trees and bushes, also disappearing from sight.

Some movement could be seen on the other side of the gate, both on the ground and in the air, but the somewhat opaque entrance made it impossible to identify what was moving in there. No sound could be heard from inside the gate, but barely visible inside were fleeting flashes of black, brown, and tan among other hues that corresponded with the various movements. The colors were swirling around, up, down, and along what seemed to the ground. What secrets were hiding behind the gate?

Suddenly, without any sound and seemingly from nowhere, an enormous grey-backed tortoise appeared on the path crawling slowly towards the outside of the gate. He looked very old as he painstakingly shuffled forward. The tortoise moved with the rising sun behind him and almost seemed to be chasing his shadow in slow motion.

As he crawled along, the old tortoise kept twisting his long neck and looking around as if he were surprised to be there or was lost. For a moment, he stopped to rest. Then after seeing the gate and staring at it for a few more moments, he again started inching forward again, heading towards that unusual structure and its shimmering opening.

# CHAPTER 2

## *DODO AND LONESOME GEORGE MEET*

**THE LARGE GREY TORTOISE** crept further along the flat dirt path to just outside the front of the metallic gate, swinging his large head from side to side as he moved, seemingly wondering where he was. He studied the gate carefully, noticing both the shimmering opening and that its three solid parts cast no shadows on the ground beyond them.

He eventually noticed the "Welcome Home, Lonesome George!" sign. He looked surprised and lumbered another step closer to the gate. As he approached it, a chirpy voice from the other side called out, "Hello, Lonesome George, come in, we've been expecting you!"

"I'm coming," Lonesome George replied as he swiveled his dark reptilian head on his long neck and peered forward trying to see who had called out to him. He couldn't see anyone through the gate and, frustrated, voiced his confusion. "Sorry whoever you are, I don't move very quickly. Who are you and how do you know who I am?"

The huge tortoise also wondered why someone expected him to come to this place and even had installed the welcome sign. He remembered that he had weighed over 165 pounds when he died at the Galapagos Islands Conservation Center

on June 24, 2012. That was about 101 years after the day he hatched on Pinta Island. While living at the Conservation Center, he often was called "the loneliest animal on the planet" because for many years he had no company from his own species even though the Center staff had searched for other tortoises related to him. Since he died, he remembered nothing except waking up a little while ago on this winding dirt path.

He took another step forward and then hesitated before going through the shimmering cloud of the strange gate. "Where am I," he asked, "And what is 'Our Forever Home?' Is it safe to come through this unusual opening? Should I just walk through?"

"Just come in, it's okay," the friendly voice replied. So Lonesome George decided to continue to crawl and moved slowly through the gate. It felt like he was pushing through thick falling rain before he could get completely through it. On the other side, he was greeted by a three-foot tall, odd-looking bird that looked like an exceptionally large turkey that also had a huge curved beak.

"Hi stranger," the unusual looking bird slightly lisped, "I'm Dodo, a flightless bird originally from an island in the Indian Ocean." Dodo had brownish-gray plumage with yellow feet, a large colorful bill, and small tail feathers. Her 25-pound weight and short height made her look chubby and clumsy, but she moved smoothly over to where Lonesome George now rested and thoroughly inspected his head, long neck, shell, and legs. They were an odd-looking pair, with small Dodo standing about 3 feet tall and Lonesome George standing about the same height on his four legs but otherwise so much larger.

"It's really me," Lonesome George snapped, irritated by Dodo's staring. "When I died, I was the last of my species anywhere in the world. I lived most of my life on Pinta Island where giant tortoises like me nearly were wiped out by sailors and pirates hunting us for food. Then the tortoises, birds, and lizards that lived there were threatened even more by humans bringing rats and other animals that ate our food and our eggs. During the last few decades, I was called a 'terminarch' because I was the last one of my kind before I died."

Dodo looked at him seriously, her smile disappearing. "We have a lot in common," she replied. "I also was the last of my species when I died in 1681, almost 350 years before your death. After I died, Dodos never were seen again except in pictures and as stuffed birds in museums, circus shows, and university collections. It's really a shame those are the only Dodo specimens left because when we were alive, we were such exceptional animals!"

She then continued to explain to Lonesome George about Dodos, strutting a little as she did so. "Although some people like to say, 'Dumb as a Dodo,' there was nothing dumb about us. We were just unlucky to be attractive to humans. In fact, because we had knees, a little-known fact, we were very agile and could move quickly across the ground. Unlike most other birds, we also had a good sense of smell. That helped us to find the freshest fruits to eat.

"But then the bad times came," she added with a sad face. "Humans not only hunted us for food like what happened to you, but also for our colorful feathers that they used to decorate their clothing. And also like what happened to you, humans added to our misery by bringing animals like pigs and rats to our island that ate our eggs and the rest of our food.

In fact, less than 100 years after humans came to the lush forests of our island of Mauritius, but about eight million years after our ancestors first flew there, they had hunted down and killed all of us, saying we were fat, lazy and stupid. The human invasion of colonists also caused the loss of virtually all the larger animals on nearby Madagascar including tortoises, giant lemurs, elephant birds, and pygmy hippopotamuses.

"Eventually, the other common human saying, 'Dead as a Dodo,' became the reality for all of us. Children today still know about us, but only because a Dodo is a character in the famous book, 'Alice in Wonderland.'"

Lonesome George was confused and shook his head slowly. He understood and sympathized with everything Dodo had explained and was sorry for her ultimate fate. Her story sounded remarkably familiar.

As he thought about Dodo, he remembered the sign outside the Galapagos conservation enclosure where he spent his last years. It said, "WHATEVER HAPPENS TO THIS SINGLE ANIMAL, LET HIM ALWAYS REMIND US THAT THE FATE OF ALL LIVING THINGS ON EARTH IS IN HUMAN HANDS." Now he understood a little better that this sign was meant to warn and teach humans about more animals than just tortoises.

Now he looked at Dodo with even more confusion on his face and thought about all the questions that were bothering him, wondering how to begin to ask them. This seemed to be the right time to find some answers.

He started by asking, "So what is this place? Where are we? Why are you and I here? Is there anyone else here? Why is it called 'Our Forever Home?'" He felt like he had a million questions that needed answering and also had not had anyone else to talk with for many years.

# CHAPTER 3

## *PASSENGER PIGEON FLIES IN*

**DODO WAS QUIET** for a moment and then sorrowfully looked over at Lonesome George and started to answer his questions. "Maybe you don't know it, but today many scientists say that five billion species of animals and plants have lived on Earth over its millions and millions of years of existence and today 99% of them are extinct. Despite these losses, there still are ten to fourteen million species of animals and plants living on the Earth even though thousands and thousands never have been seen or named by humans.

"For all the animals and plants that became extinct, this place, 'Our Forever Home,' is their new forever home, a final permanent resting place. Here is where the last one of each of us goes after extinction, to live safely forever with our memories of better days. Here we are away from today's humans, away from the unhealthy and dangerous conditions on Earth, and protected from any predators.

"But there's a very important catch," she added. "Because each of us is the very last one of our species, we never will have any mates or children. Most of the animals here have learned to live together with each other in peace without threats or attacks. That's because we don't want to be like humans and because we don't want to kill the last of

a species again," she finished, slowly shaking her head. As she stood there and thought for a moment, a small shadow slowly floated over their heads.

Dodo instantly flashed a big smile on her face and her eyes lit up. "Oh, look up there, here's my best friend in Our Forever Home!" she exclaimed. "Lonesome George, meet Passenger Pigeon! Passenger Pigeon, come on down here and meet our newest resident!"

Passenger Pigeon lazily flew around the two of them. Her shiny grey neck feathers and her bright red breast feathers fluttered in the breeze, all in sharp contrast to the bright blue sky over her. She floated down and landed on a branch near Dodo and Lonesome George and meticulously primped and preened her feathers. She finally finished, cocked her head, and looked carefully at the new visitor. "I know you, you're the famous tortoise from the Galapagos Islands who lived alone for many years and recently died," she squawked with a harsh voice.

Then without a further word, she stopped gazing at them, flapped her long wings, and soared back up in the air, again showing off all her bright feathers. She circled around them in a widening circle as she continued to talk to Lonesome George.

"When I heard you were coming, I started to think about my old days and about all the other Passenger Pigeons. Our story unfortunately was like both of yours. Passenger Pigeons once survived for many generations, in fact for over 100,000 years. I was the last Passenger Pigeon alive after the remaining few wild Passenger Pigeons were killed by human hunters in about 1901. I was born in the Cincinnati Zoo and was named Martha by my keepers. I died in captivity at the zoo on September 1,1914, after living my entire 29-year life there.

"Passenger Pigeons were amazing birds," she bragged with her raspy voice. "We were over a foot long and could fly over 60 miles an hour. We also were beautiful, just like I am today. We lived mostly in eastern North America and there were three to five billion of us—yes, billion with a 'b'--roosting in various forested places when Europeans first arrived on the continent."

She then laughed and continued to boast, "When Passenger Pigeons migrated each year, our flocks were so long and wide that the skies got dark and it sometimes took over a dozen hours for a single flock to pass over a town or river. That's like all night or all day!"

Lonesome George looked at her with surprise on his face and asked, "If there were so many of you, why did your species disappear? And couldn't you do anything to prevent your extinction?"

"Believe it or not, what happened to us occurred for many of the same reasons that caused yours and Dodo's extinctions. And no, we couldn't do anything about it," Passenger Pigeon retorted angrily. "We were hunted and shot by humans because we provided cheap meat. Also, humans often destroyed our roosting areas and nests by chopping down the forests where we lived so that they could build farms and towns for themselves.

"Destroying the forests took away both our protection and our food sources. Humans also brought along with them various animals that hunted or harassed us. We eventually realized that we were particularly vulnerable due to of one of our unique habits. Unlike most other birds, Passenger Pigeons lived communally in large areas. Because so many of us lived together, we were easy to find and hunt. But, of course, we couldn't change that basic habit or stop the humans' intrusions so we all died eventually," she finished.

Lonesome George frowned, thinking that it was odd that he and both of his new friends had suffered from similar problems caused by humans and eventually ended up with the same final consequences. He knew about some efforts in the Galapagos Islands to save various animals and birds from the problems caused by humans, but he didn't realize how great a problem this had been in other parts of the world. It seemed like these troubles had existed for many years longer than he could have imagined. He wondered out loud how many other times these problems had hurt various other animals, as well as fish, insects, and plants.

# CHAPTER 4

## *BLACK RHINOCEROS STOMPS BY*

**THE ANSWER CAME QUICKLY.** As Passenger Pigeon was about to start describing other birds that had become extinct, she was interrupted by loud thrashing in the bushes nearby them. Only a very large animal moving through the underbrush and coming towards them could create so much noise. Lonesome George could not move quickly enough to get out of the way so as the sounds of the approaching animal got closer, he immediately pulled his head, neck, and legs back into his shell for protection.

"Don't worry, you're not in danger," a deep voice intoned slowly as a huge dark animal stopped nearby them. "I'm just West African Black Rhinoceros and I wanted to meet our famous new guest. Howdy, new friend! Or as they say in Kenya, 'Jambo!'"

"Wow," Lonesome George exclaimed as he slowly scooted his head forward and peeked upwards out of his shell, "You're the biggest blackest animal I've ever seen! You must be at least six feet tall and weigh over a ton!"

"That's right," Black Rhinoceros answered. "I am that big, and by the way, some of my old friends and relatives weighed up to three tons. But you shouldn't be fooled. I may be odd looking with my large body, two horns and thick, hard wrinkly skin but don't let my looks deceive you into

underestimating me. I also may not look very athletic, but I can run 35 miles an hour if I'm charging you or running away from something that scares me.

"Rhinoceroses over time came in various sizes and colors. You're right, Lonesome George, I'm black like some of my relatives but there are others who are gray, brown, red, or white. We're not considered the smartest of all animals, but we can hold our own with most of them."

He shook his head, just missing Dodo with one of his two horns, and then apologized, "Sorry, Dodo, I sometimes forget that my front curved horn is over two feet long. But it's useful to dig up roots as well as to defend myself or scare away predators who threaten me."

Dodo always seemed to have something more to add to a conversation and jumped in to say to Lonesome George, "I'll tell you something else you should know since we just were talking about birds. While I'm only a friend of his here, other birds had a really special relationship with the West African Black Rhinoceros. He has a good sense of hearing and of smell but has very bad eyesight and only can see about 40 feet away. Because of his bad eyes, and in order to protect himself, the Black Rhinoceros often relied on birds being startled by something that might be threatening him and they chirped or squawked to warn him.

"He also can't reach around or scratch himself when ticks and flies bother him because of his thick neck and short tail. But that's not a problem because one of my cousins, the Oxpecker Bird, actually lived on Black Rhinoceros and fed itself on the pests that lived in cracks of his skin."

"Well, all of that makes it sound like you really could take care of yourself," Lonesome George responded thoughtfully and then he asked, "So what happened to you and why are you here in Our Forever Home? Were you too big to find enough food for yourself? Or did something else happen to kill all your species?"

"No, I wasn't too big," growled Black Rhinoceros, "But I wasn't very respected by humans. From what I understand, we suffered from many of the same threats and problems that all three of you had to deal with. Now that humans are everywhere on Earth, it seems to be a common theme even though various types of rhinoceroses have been around for almost 5 million years longer than them. Imagine, there were over a million rhinoceroses at the beginning of the 1800's, but I was the last West African Black Rhinoceros when I died in 2011."

He hesitated and took a couple deep breaths to calm his growing irritation. "You asked why did we all finally die? For one thing, humans cleared the areas we lived in for their farming and firewood and then we no longer could browse in the bushes for our food. We also were hunted for sport, but that's not the worst of it. Many Chinese humans believed that our body parts were good medicines, especially powdered rhinoceros horns. So often we were killed just for our horns to be cut off and ground up and the rest of our bodies were left for animal scavengers."

Black Rhinoceros shook his head in disgust and continued his story. "Even though we could live for 30 years, Black Rhinoceros females were able to have a baby only once every two-and-a-half to three years, so we needed to have a large stable population. But our population growth was threatened and reduced by too much hunting and deforestation of our home habitats. Eventually, most of our safe places to live and browse either disappeared or were found by hunters. Finally, the obvious happened: no more mothers and babies and then no more West African Black Rhinoceroses."

Lonesome George looked astounded at his three hosts. "I'm beginning to see a trend here that I only knew a little about before I died. Now I want to know more. Have these human problems causing extinctions been around for a long time, or are they just getting more serious throughout the world during the last several hundred years?" he asked.

"Actually, the various types of harm caused by humans have existed for many, many centuries, in some cases ever since humans first appeared on Earth hundreds of thousands of years ago," Dodo immediately answered, becoming more serious again. "But lately it seems that I'm greeting more and more individual species of animals arriving at Our Forever Home than I ever did before. New arrivals are coming here almost every week and sometimes more often than that.

"Also, I am constantly hearing dire warnings from some of the new arrivals about how many other species are dwindling in numbers and then being identified as threatened or critically endangered. It seems like overwhelming numbers of hazards are killing our fellow animals without anybody doing much about the problems or for these creatures!"

Dodo thought for a moment and then added, "I don't want you to think of me as a 'Debbie Downer,' the one who always has the bad news and negative outlooks. But here's another important piece of information to put all of this in context. Just since 1900, over 500 species of animals alone have become extinct, not even counting insects and spiders and plants.

"Looking at this growing catastrophe another way, scientists have said that since 1700, over 320 mammals have become extinct. In addition, at least a quarter of all vertebrates, animals with backbones, are at risk of extinction including 40% of all amphibians, 33% of marine mammals, 31% of sharks and rays, 25% of mammals, and 14% of birds.

"The Wide World Foundation recently described the deteriorating status of wildlife as 'staggering' and said this trend shows 'an absolute disrespect for animals and the environment.' That group has a global biodiversity index that estimates an average 68% decrease in population sizes of mammals, birds, amphibians, reptiles, and fish between 1970 and 2016.

"The same report says there is a lot of blame to go around. Population declines by region showed that 94% were in Latin America and the Caribbean, 65% were in Africa, 45% were in Asia-Pacific, 33% were in North America, and 24% were in Europe and Central Asia. These catastrophic losses might not seem that obvious to most humans on Earth today, but they add up quickly, especially because they're happening more and more often as each year goes by," she finished.

Passenger Pigeon then swooped over and added another final thought. "Fortunately, or unfortunately, depending on your viewpoint, Our Forever Home is huge and is undisturbed by humans. Because of that, we have room for the millions of species that have disappeared during the entire history of the world, many even before humans came along, and we still have room for the millions more who are likely to become extinct in the future. It is truly a 'forever home.'" She then nodded her head to Black Rhinoceros for him to continue explaining to Lonesome George about Our Forever Home.

# CHAPTER 5

## *CATS LIVED MANY LIVES*

**AFTER A MOMENT OF SILENCE**, Black Rhinoceros looked down at Lonesome George and, with his slow deep voice, resumed his explanation. “Now that you live here, you'll have lots of time in the future to look around all of Our Forever Home. Even though you move slowly, there are ways to see everything, meet everyone, and learn about each of the animals’ stories. You also will be able to see all the different animals in their own original time periods and habitats where they lived before they became extinct. They all live in conditions they are familiar with and with other animals they previously knew. In fact, soon we’re going to take you to meet some of them.”

Black Rhinoceros continued his description without any more hesitation. “We have many types of animals here in Our Forever Home. Even though you already are acquainted with cats because they pestered you in the Galapagos Islands, you soon will learn that a really wide variety of cats already are living here.

“Because you previously only knew about small cats, you especially should take advantage of the opportunity to meet larger cats like the Tasmanian Tiger that now lives here. It was a unique cat that looked more like a yellow-brown dog and had zebra stripes on its back and large claws on its feet.

It measured about four feet long with a two-foot long tail and weighed about 60 to 70 pounds. But despite its name, the Tasmanian Tiger was quite different from most other cats.

"For one thing," he explained, "Even though it was related to the loud and ferocious Tasmanian Devil, the Tasmanian Tiger was shy and mostly moved around and hunted at night rather than during the day. Also, it both could hop like a kangaroo as well as run. The Tasmanian Tiger's other unique feature was that both the males and females had pouches like a kangaroo, but the openings of the pouches faced towards the animals' back ends instead of towards their heads. The females carried their young, called 'joeys,' for up to about 3 months.

"The Tasmanian Tiger is believed to have appeared on Earth first about two million years ago, during what scientists call the Early Pleistocene Epoch. Its ancestors were even older, going back 23 million years to the Miocene Epoch. Eventually, and I hate to sound like a broken record, it was hunted to extinction by human farmers and bounty hunters, and the last one known to be alive was killed in 1936.

"Another interesting large cat here is the Caspian Tiger from Central Asia," Black Rhinoceros added. "It wasn't as big as I am but was one of the largest cats that ever existed. Ours living here has a body over nine feet long and in addition has a three-foot tail. With all that, it weighs about 300 pounds! What happened to its species? One guess! Humans hunted it for sport because it was so large and had a gorgeous pelt. But, finally, its complete extinction was ordered by the Russian government for one reason, to clear land for expanding agriculture, especially cotton plantations."

Black Rhinoceros smiled before he continued, saying that we always can find some irony in our various histories. "We all know that despite what I just described to two large cats, many humans treat some cats as cherished and pampered pets and once they even considered them to be gods.

"For example, in early Egypt, Ra, the Sun God, was the parent of the cat god, Bastet, sometimes known as 'Bast.' Bastet was one of the most important Egyptian gods and the companion of the high goddess Isis. A lesser Egyptian cat god was Sekhmet, usually pictured as a lioness, who was the goddess of war.

"Can you imagine, as early as 450 B.C., the penalty for killing a cat was death, and ancient Egyptians even embalmed and buried their cats in sacred vessels? They were not the earliest cat worshippers either: a cat skeleton dating to 9,500 B.C. was found carefully buried on the Island of Cyprus.

"After the early Egyptian historical times, cat worship continued throughout the ages. The Chinese worshipped the cat god Li Shou that protected crops from being eaten by rats and mice. Also, a Pre-Incan civilization worshipped Ai-Apaec, an old man with long fangs and cat whiskers who came from an ancient cat god and could take the form of a tomcat.

"Later, the Greeks worshipped their goddess Hecate who assumed the form of a cat for protection, and the Norse goddess Freyja rode in a chariot with two large grey cats given to her by Thor, the mightiest of the Norse gods. Those two cats were revered as sources of good fortune for fertile crops. Other special cats appear in the literature of ancient India and Persia, early Egypt and Rome, and also among Native Americans.

"Despite that history of love and respect, many early and still-living large wild cats have been treated as pests or hazards instead of as cherished friends or with care, and they constantly have been killed or otherwise eliminated," Black Rhinoceros grunted. "Those cats that were neither pets nor pests had few other uses for humans. They were valued only for their skins or sometimes for their body parts to be used like my horns for medicines.

"What I find really amazing and disgusting is one kind of behavior. Although today's humans consider themselves more 'civilized' than earlier humans, they actively still participate in sport hunting of large cats just so they can show off the stuffed head of a dead large cat as a trophy on one of their home or office walls.

"Of course, where there are cats, you'll always also find dogs, mice, and other common animals," Black Rhinoceros added with a smile. "I'm sure as you wander around here you'll see all types of animals that were ancestors of those you used to know."

At that point, Passenger Pigeon landed on a rock nearby and started preening again. She was bored with all the talk about cats, not her favorite animal, and added, "Yes, in Our Forever Home, you'll see or hear about every type of living creature that has existed on Earth for at least a while during the past hundreds of millions of years. You will be introduced to animals that have become extinct just in the last year, decade, or century as well as those who died millions of years ago. We also will talk about many of the living relatives of previously extinct animals that now are endangered or at imminent risk of extinction and soon may come to live here.

"Our Forever Home has many animals you probably have heard of, but also is occupied by thousands of animals living in the air, land, or sea that humans never knew existed. I'm sure you'll be both impressed and excited to start living and traveling here," she finished and flew up over them again.

Having heard this initial description of Our Forever Home, Lonesome George became curious and interrupted to ask, "Black Rhinoceros, I can see a river over there near the hills. I assume you also have oceans and lakes here in Our Forever Home for water animals and fish?" He remembered his days at the Galapagos Islands and all the animals like seals and sea lions he would see by the hundreds swimming in the ocean or lying in the sun on beaches. "So, do you have seals and other water mammals here?"

# CHAPTER 6

## *WATER MAMMALS AND FROGS SWARM*

**"OF COURSE WE HAVE OCEANS,** and lakes, rivers, and other places with water too," answered Black Rhinoceros. "Our Forever Home is the final home for many extinct water mammals like seals and whales as well as many types of reptiles, amphibians, and fish who lived in or near Earth's rivers, lakes and oceans.

"I don't know if you know this but the first creatures to live on the Earth four and one-half billion years ago originally lived in the oceans, and an amazing variety of water creatures have evolved there ever since. Later we will tell you more about these creatures and how some of them also evolved to move from land into the oceans and how others evolved to move from water to land. Also, over time, you will meet many of your own ancient ancestors as well as more recently extinct relatives.

"Let me answer your question about seals and other water mammals at Our Forever Home," he continued. "I'll describe a few of them for you. One of our residents here is a Caribbean Monk Seal. The earliest sightings of this seal by Europeans were by Christopher Columbus in 1494 and a couple decades later they were seen again in the Caribbean by the Spanish explorer, Ponce de Leon. They've been around for a long time!

"Unfortunately, these seals later were killed by the hundreds for their blubber which was used by humans for fuel oil and food. Over time, due to human overfishing, the seals' habitats also lost the fish and mollusks they needed as food to survive. The last Caribbean Monk Seals were seen in the early 1950's. One is here now because that variety of seal was declared extinct in 2008.

"Another of our more impressive aquatic neighbors is the Japanese Sea Lion. It first appeared on Earth about two million years ago during the Early Pleistocene Epoch. Those sea lions really were something to see! They were up to eight feet long and weighed over half a ton, far larger than their current California cousins. The meat of the Japanese Sea Lion was not very tasty to eat. However, it also was hunted for its skins to be used for leather goods, for its fat to be used for oil lamp fuel, for its internal organs to be used for Asian medicines, and even for its whiskers to be used for pipe cleaners. Because of overhunting, only a few dozen remained alive by the early 1930's and a living Japanese Sea Lion has not been seen since about 1974. They now are seen only as taxidermized examples in several museums."

Black Rhinoceros paused to think of other marine mammals he had seen in water sites at Our Forever Home. "There is also a Baiji White Dolphin here, sometimes called the Yangtze River Dolphin, that lived only in China's Yangtze River. This dolphin originally had a very special status because it was considered the goddess of protection by local boatmen and fishermen. It grew to be about eight feet long and weighed up to a quarter of a ton.

"Although these Baiji White Dolphins had tiny eyes and bad eyesight, they survived successfully for 20 million years until their river habitats were destroyed. How and why were these habitats destroyed? Because the Yangtze River was used for so many other purposes that were dangerous to the dolphins such as fishing, transportation, and damming for hydroelectricity. Those intrusions into their natural habitats decimated the Baiji White Dolphin population and they haven't been seen anywhere since 2002 except for the last one here in Our Forever Home."

Dodo interrupted after that story and said it was important for Lonesome George to think about other water animals too. "I also know a lot about water animals," she remarked. "In addition to eating seeds, nuts and fruit, Dodos ate from the water too, especially shellfish and crabs. But that's not the only reason I have something else to say.

"You may not have noticed, Lonesome George, but Black Rhinoceros hasn't said anything yet about amphibians, another major water-based type of animal that has been on Earth for about 370 million years since the Devonian Period. They are important for many reasons including that they were the first animals to live on land after slowly migrating away from the seas. Even today they spend part of their lives in water and part on land. In fact, their name comes from the Greek word 'amphibios' which means 'both kinds of life,' referring to their dual water-land life cycles.

"While there are many stories about amphibians that I could tell you, I remember most vividly one I heard recently from a new arrival. The Rabb's Fringe-Limbed Treefrog first was discovered in the Panama rainforest in 2005. It was about three inches long and had huge beautiful brown eyes and very large feet. This treefrog was unique because to avoid predators on the ground it could glide from tree to tree by spreading its large, webbed feet and front legs. It also was special because it was the only known frog that allowed its young tadpoles to eat the skin from the father's back in order to survive. Most of this treefrog species died because of a fungus infection that spread through their entire small habitat. The last known Rabb's Fringe-Limbed Treefrog died in a zoo in 2016, just eleven years after being discovered. Like you and Passenger Pigeon, it had a name, 'Toughie.'

"Sadly, in the last 20 years, out of the 8,000 species of living amphibians known to humans, almost 170 species of toads, frogs, newts, and salamanders have become extinct. This has happened mostly because of the loss of their living areas in or near water due to humans' land development. Also, climate change is causing unhealthy high temperatures and sicknesses. Finally, many also have been harvested by humans for food, pets, and medicinal purposes and those uses continue today.

"The Gastric Incubator Frog was another tiny amphibian that was fascinating because it had a unique reproductive system. Originally from Queensland, Australia, the female frog swallowed her fertilized eggs and incubated them in her stomach. After six weeks, the baby frogs were fully developed and entered the world by coming back out through the mother's mouth. This frog has been considered extinct since 2000."

Lonesome George looked at her in surprise. "It seems like a lot of these amphibians are dying off in a very short period of time. Why is that happening? Can't anyone do anything about it?"

"I'm glad you asked why amphibians are becoming extinct at such a great rate," Dodo responded. "It's because of their unique biology: they live part of their lives in water and part on land. As a result, any significant changes in either one of those habitats can interfere with their reproduction, growth, and health. That interference then causes their populations to quickly crash. Also, you were saved for a while when you were moved from your island to the Galapagos Conservancy, but most amphibians cannot be moved to other places. Once their habitats are destroyed for development or agriculture, they cannot be replaced. As a result, they are extremely sensitive to both general changes in the climate as well as the various changes caused by humans."

As Lonesome George, Black Rhinoceros, and Dodo were talking, with Passenger Pigeon gliding overhead, they were slowly wandering along a small dirt path leading further into the interior of Our Forever Home. Just as he had imagined from outside the gate, Lonesome George could see large and small trees, low hills rising to high mountains, waving grasses, and spreads of beautiful multi-colored flowers and shrubbery. He also could see footprints and other indications of other animals living there, and now knew that he eventually also would see lakes, rivers, and other water habitats. He already was sure that this place was far more interesting than his former enclosure at the Galapagos Islands Conservation Center. As an additional benefit, he now had new animal friends to keep him company.

# CHAPTER 7

## *TURTLES, TORTOISES TIME TRAVEL*

**"YOU KNOW, WE HAVEN'T TALKED** much about your turtle species," Dodo said to Lonesome George. "When we meet new friends here, we love to tell them about our own histories and those of our ancestors, as you'll find out soon. How much do you know about the past of your own species and how humans felt about or related to turtles?"

"I'm not just a 'turtle,' I'm a 'tortoise,'" Lonesome George quickly responded, chastising Dodo's choice of labeling. "Other than that, I learned some things about tortoises and turtles when I lived on the Galapagos Island where I was born and then later in captivity. What do you know about them, Dodo?"

"Ha! I knew you'd complain about being called a 'turtle,'!" Dodo replied. "But a 'tortoise' is merely a land turtle as opposed to a water turtle. In the same way I've learned about a lot about the other animals here, I've become almost an expert on turtles and tortoises too because many types of them live in Our Forever Home and have talked about themselves. You tortoises really have a very fascinating history, and I'm going to tell you about some of it. That way, you'll be able to share it later with other animals you meet here," she started to explain.

"Did you know, for example, that the ancestors of turtles and tortoises date back over 260 million years ago to the Late Permian Epoch? And that unlike you, those turtle ancestors had teeth? But they didn't have either your top shell, called a 'carapace,' nor your front or bottom shell, called a 'plastron.' The first turtle ancestor with a plastron evolved about 220 million years ago, and the carapace came later."

"As you can tell, size is something I always can relate to," Black Rhinoceros interjected. "I know something about your larger ancestors. The largest ever sea turtle lived about 66 million years ago during the Late Cretaceous Period. It was called Archelon and was about 15 feet long, 13 feet from flipper edge to flipper edge, and weighed almost 5,000 pounds. The largest freshwater turtle was called Stupendemys. It lived during the Miocene Epoch, about 13 million to five million years ago and was almost 10 feet long with a weight of about 2,500 pounds.

"You can compare those sizes to today's largest living turtle, your cousin the Leatherback Sea Turtle, which only is about six and a half feet long and weighs 'only' about 1,500 pounds. However, this living cousin of yours has developed many other special characteristics.

"Its front flippers are flat and can be as much as nine feet long, helping it to swim more effectively in the ocean. These large flippers also allow it to pursue its favorite food, jellyfish. It can swim up to 20 miles an hour and can dive up to 4,000 feet deep for as long as an hour to find and eat them. While foraging for food, Pacific Leatherback Turtles will travel about 6,000 miles across the Pacific from their nesting grounds in Asia to eat California jellyfish. Amazingly, one

Leatherback Turtle was tracked for over 12,000 miles during 647 days of travel.

"Sadly, the Leatherback Sea Turtle's overall population is declining rapidly due to a variety of factors, one of the most serious of which is they eat plastic bags they find floating in the ocean. They mistake these floating plastic bags for jellyfish and when they eat them, the bags don't dissolve and then block their digestive tracts. This eventually causes them to starve to death. The Pacific Leatherback Sea Turtle is one of the most endangered turtle populations on Earth with only about 2,000 adult females remaining for males to mate with.

"Besides their large size," Black Rhinoceros continued, "The long life spans of tortoises are quite astounding. Giant land tortoises existed throughout much of the world in prehistoric times. However, after the appearance of humans, they generally became extinct everywhere except in the Galapagos and Seychelles Islands. The tortoises there can live up to 150 years or longer.

"I'm not sure you ever heard of her but, as an example, a tortoise named 'Harriet' was believed to have been brought to England in 1875 by Charles Darwin on his famous ship, the Beagle. Later, she was moved to and lived in the Queensland Zoo from 1987 until her death in 2007 at the estimated age of 176 years old."

Lonesome George nodded his large head in response to what they both had said and replied that he could tell them some even more interesting information about turtles and tortoises. "Did you know we're quite intelligent and can be taught tasks we then can remember for years? For example, rather than having to dig, tortoises stomp on the ground to get worms to come up so that we can eat them after less effort. We also have excellent night vision, good color vision, and communicate with a variety of sounds. It is generally believed that these sounds help our groups stay together when we're migrating.

"That's not all. Over time, our bodies have adapted in many ways to improve our lives. Our shells protect us from animals trying to harm or kill us. Since we cannot move fast, we can snap our heads and necks quickly around to catch prey in our beaks or to attack predators. Some turtles can stay underwater for up to an hour to hunt or hide. And we live longer lives than most other animals because our internal organs, like lungs and kidneys, do not age or deteriorate over time."

Lonesome George smiled and told them that he also was proud of the important role turtles played in religious beliefs. "Hindus refer to us as 'Kurma,' a god related to the Hindu god Vishnu. The ancient priests say Kurma also is directly related to the 'World-Turtle' that usually is seen in old religious texts carrying the Earth on its back shell. In some world mythology, the tortoise even is related to the creator of all living things including plants, and the slow withdrawal and extension of a turtle's legs is believed to represent self-control and detachment."

Dodo interrupted, looking seriously at Lonesome George, and said she had to relate some less favorable information. "That's all very interesting. However, like many other animals, turtles have both 'good news' stories like the ones you told us about and 'bad news' stories that I have to tell you about.

"Did you know that turtles weren't always considered to be friendly, beneficial, or sacred animals? During the time of the Greek Empire, a tortoise was the symbol of the Greek god Hermes who was described as a trickster and the protector of thieves, among others. During the Roman Empire, the pre-Christian cult of Mithras believed that turtles were symbolic of darkness as opposed to goodness and light.

"Later, during early Christian history, turtles symbolized evil and heresy because they were low to the ground and wallowed in mud and dirt. Even the word 'turtle' itself is derived from a Latin phrase referring to 'infernal beast,' a reference to hell or the devil.

"The other bad news I need to point out relates to what you said earlier about being hunted. Turtle flesh still is enjoyed in many cultures as a main ingredient in both turtle soup and turtle stew. In fact, today there are turtle farms to raise sea turtles, freshwater turtles, and land tortoises just for their meat. Also, I bet you didn't know that turtle fat is used in Central America as a primary ingredient in cosmetics. And finally, similar to the problem Black Rhinoceros had, turtle plastrons are ground up and used in traditional Chinese medicines."

Lonesome George groaned because those "bad news" stories created a dark cloud over continuing to talk about turtles and tortoises. Now, he wanted to start moving again and talk about and see other creatures.

As they moved forward, he saw head of them was a flat grassy clearing with rolling low shrubbery and a few trees scattered around. When he looked carefully in any direction, he could see numerous small animals scurrying on the ground and a variety of birds soaring or floating in the sky. All around them was a peaceful and colorful place with plenty of activity and a lot to learn about.

# CHAPTER 8

## *BIRDS COME AND GO*

**AS THEY STARTED TO WALK** again in silence, Dodo took over Black Rhinoceros' introduction for Lonesome George. "You've met Passenger Pigeon and me, but Our Forever Home is full of many other types of birds. Some of them first existed long before the beginning of mammal time and became extinct throughout the centuries. Then other species of birds appeared after them and even some of these became extinct more recently. All of the extinct birds disappeared for many of the same reasons we've already talked about, as well as because of other problems that we'll talk about later."

Dodo said she wanted to tell him about one of her favorite birds living in Our Forever Home. "Did you know there was a bird in New Zealand called the Laughing Owl?" she asked. "It had yellow-brown feathers and even had feathers on its talons. Instead of chirping, its laugh was like the barking of a small dog, although the Laughing Owl also hooted or chattered when it was flying. It chased ground animals for food, catching them by running on the ground rather than by flying and diving like other birds of prey. The Laughing Owl disappeared when its natural habitats were replaced by human land development, and because humans

brought to New Zealand other animals which scientists refer to as 'invasive species' that preyed on the Laughing Owls."

Passenger Pigeon reappeared over their heads and interrupted, "It's my turn! I just have to add something I know about! I don't know what it's like in the Galapagos Islands, but just in the Hawaiian Islands there were about 70 unique native birds. Unfortunately, about half of them now are either extinct or believed to be extinct. A similar problem has happened on the island of Guam where 60 percent of its native bird species have become extinct in the last 30 years, mostly due to humans' introduction of the brown tree snake.

"One of the saddest stories for me is what happened to the Hawaiian O'o. It was a cherished bird because it had a long, striking feathered tail and large beautiful yellow feathers on its wings. Over the years, native Hawaiians had been careful with them and without killing the O'o's had plucked only a few of their feathers at a time for ceremonial robes and capes. Afterwards, they released the birds to continue to live. But later, European colonists arrived on the islands and hunted and killed them by the hundreds for display collections and sport. Eventually, none survived.

"I could tell you about many more birds that now live here," she said and frowned as she continued, "But one of the most versatile and misunderstood birds in Our Forever Home is the late Great Auk. It was about three feet tall and weighed about nine pounds, about the same size as a human baby. It could swim and dive as well as fly. After being hunted extensively throughout Europe, the only Great Auk colony eventually remaining was located on an isolated island near Iceland. Then the last of these wonderful birds was killed in Scotland in 1844 when three men thought it was a witch that was causing a large storm.

"The Great Auk soon may have company here from one of its relatives, the Puffin," Passenger Pigeon continued. "Humans think that Puffins are enchantingly cute, and their pictures can be seen in many nature and travel magazines. They live along the coastlines in both the north Atlantic and north Pacific Oceans and have red and black large beaks, orange legs, and black-and-white body plumage.

"These plumage colors are the reason for their scientific name. The Puffin is one species in the genus 'fratercula,' which translates to 'friar.' This scientific name was given to Puffins because of their body feathers' black-and-white colors that looked like a friar's cowl.

"Puffins are about a foot long and can walk on their hind legs like penguins, paddle when they swim in the ocean for their food, and fly using their two-foot wingspans when they're hunting or looking for safety. They don't squawk when they are flying, they just make a sound like a purr. I really hope we don't see the last Puffin very soon," she finished.

As Passenger Pigeon was about to tell another story, Dodo started fidgeting, indicating that she was anxious to contribute another one of her own stories. "I'm sure you know there are many nonflying birds like ostriches and emus in the world, both today and in the past. One of the early nonflying birds was the Stirton's Thunderbird that was about 10 feet tall and weighed about 1,100 pounds. It was one of the largest feathered birds ever discovered. It lived in

Australia during the late Miocene Epoch, about 30 million years ago.

"The Thunderbird had strong legs and an extremely powerful large beak. That led some scientists to believe that it was a carnivore, adding to the reasons some also called it 'The Demon Duck of Doom.' The last imprints of its footprints date back to about 30,000 years ago, not coincidentally soon after the arrival of the first humans in Australia about 48,000 to 60,000 years ago."

"You know, I never knew how widespread these problems with humans were," Lonesome George remarked as he looked at the others seriously. "I always lived either isolated on my island or alone. I know this is hard to talk about but tell me, Dodo, Passenger Pigeon, and Black Rhinoceros, what other kinds of animals have become extinct because of all this interference caused by humans?"

# CHAPTER 9

## *INSECTS CAN'T SURVIVE EITHER*

**PASSENGER PIGEON FLEW BACK DOWN** again and after a little more preening, said she would tell Lonesome George about some of these other animals and what happened to them. She explained that because she could fly everywhere in Our Forever Home and had very good eyesight, she had seen and talked with many of the smaller animals and insects that have disappeared from Earth in the past.

"I can tell you so many stories about their difficult lives and unfortunate endings," she whined. "If you look carefully as you wander and explore around here, you will see a lot of very small living things like insects, snails, spiders, moths, and other invertebrates. If you didn't know it, 'invertebrates' are animals that do not have a backbone or spine.

"Eventually you may meet our Madeiran Large White Butterfly. It is about three inches long and has pure white wings except for black tips and is more than twice that in length. It lived on an island called Madeira south of Portugal and it was the first known European butterfly to become extinct. That happened because its habitat was destroyed by humans' construction of homes and businesses as well as because of humans' use of agricultural chemicals and introduction of a predatory virus.

"Another beautiful lost butterfly is the Xerces Blue that lived in the coastal areas of San Francisco," she continued. "It had gorgeous blue wings with white spots. In the 1940's it was believed to be the first American butterfly species to become extinct. That happened also because of rampant human land development that destroyed the coastal vegetation this butterfly lived on.

"Here's an interesting insect you'll run across one day," Passenger Pigeon remarked. "The largest insect ever known was an insect called Meganeura that resembled a dragonfly. It had a three-foot wingspan, just imagine a yardstick, and was a foot-and-a-half long! It existed before birds or even flying reptiles appeared, about 300 million years ago during the Carboniferous Period. When you see it, you'll recognize it not only because of its size but also because it has very large eyes and has hooks on its legs to capture the other insects it preyed on and ate."

"Not all extinct insects were flyers," Dodo countered. "An ancestor of the cockroach called Manipulator crawled around on Earth about 94 million years ago. It had long legs that it used both to chase and to grab its food. I'm sure you've heard that cockroaches and their immediate ancestors have been on Earth for almost 280 million years since the Carboniferous Period.

"Cockroaches have been able to survive for this long because they constantly are evolving special features like being able to live without a head because they breathe through holes in their body segments. Without a head they finally die after a week only because they can't drink water without a mouth. They also can run or skitter up to three miles an hour and hold their breaths for up to 40 minutes. The largest living cockroach is six inches long with a 12-inch wingspan! Because cockroaches are so versatile and adaptable, many humans believe that they may survive on Earth long after even humans become extinct.

"Here's another interesting insect example! The Arthropluera was a giant millipede which is more like a spider than an insect. Before it became extinct, it was the largest invertebrate ever to live on Earth. It stretched almost nine feet long and lived in North America and Scotland during the Carboniferous Period, 345 million to 295 million years ago. Its body had about 30 jointed segments with over 8 legs on each segment. Just imagine, it had over 240 legs! It was not a carnivore and had few predators since it was so large. It became extinct soon after the Carboniferous Period when the climate dried out and reduced both the rainforests it lived in and the food it relied on there to survive."

Black Rhinoceros then interrupted and said, "Let me add a sad coincidence that I didn't mention before when we were talking about marine mammals. There used to be an insect called the Caribbean Monk Seal Nasal Mite that lived in the noses of only Caribbean Monk Seals. Unfortunately, when the Caribbean Monk Seal became extinct, this Nasal Mite also became extinct.

"A similar thing could happen to the Sword-Billed Hummingbird. This bird relies on long-tubed passionflowers for its nectar to eat and in exchange pollinates those flowers. What do you think will happen if either one of them suffers significant losses or becomes extinct?"

He then looked at the others and said he had one more unfortunate African small creature to talk about. "Once upon a time there was a Lake Pedder Earthworm discovered only in Tasmania. In fact, this earthworm lived only on the sandy shores of Lake Pedder and seemed to be an interesting invertebrate when it was discovered in 1971 because of some of its unique features. It was about two inches long but had almost 130 segments. Each worm was both a male and female and could mate with any other Lake Pedder Earthworm. Unfortunately, it couldn't be studied carefully or for very long because it disappeared forever one year later when the Lake Pedder area deliberately was flooded to build a hydroelectric facility."

"Throughout the world," Passenger Pigeon sighed, "Hundreds, if not thousands, of types of butterflies, moths, crickets and grasshoppers, beetles, and dragonflies, among other insects, have disappeared forever and now are found only here in Our Forever Home. According to today's scientists, almost half of all insect species are declining and a third are endangered. In fact, the insect rate of extinction is eight times faster than that of mammals, reptiles and birds! Another way of looking at this growing problem is that 10% of the total weight and number of insects is lost forever every 4 years.

"Some insects are being lost due to climate change, some from harm caused naturally by other creatures, and many others because of human interference caused by the use of pesticides, by agriculture that removes trees and shrubs they live in, and by urbanization that eliminates other habitats. The impacts of these insect losses effect everything on earth, ranging from the various animals that eat insects in order to survive to the work insects do to pollinate, clean dead matter, and eliminate other insects that are pests."

Dodo shuffled her feet, gazed into the sky, and thought about all the flying insects she had seen up there as well as those scurrying on the ground, swimming in ponds and lakes, and burrowing underground. When Passenger Pigeon paused, Dodo repeated her earlier complaint, "Just like with other animals, this insect problem isn't only an ancient historical issue. We'll talk more at some point about the terrible things that humans still are doing today to insects, even to important ones like bees."

Lonesome George looked around again and noticed a lizard basking in the warm sun on a large nearby boulder. He wondered about it, and then asked out loud, "That lizard is a reptile. Tortoises like me are reptiles. Can you tell me some of the history of reptiles that are living here other than turtles?"

# CHAPTER 10

## *REPTILES ARE DISAPPEARING TOO*

**DODO WAS PREPARED** for that question because she had seen where Lonesome George was staring and so she could answer immediately. "I'll tell you about the evolution and lives of some recent and older reptiles. Some of them you've heard of but others are not as well-known.

"Like the other animals we already have mentioned, many famous and not-so-famous reptiles, both large and small, also have appeared on and disappeared from Earth over the years. Reptiles and their ancestors date back all the way to prehistoric times and include the famous dinosaurs you have heard of and that we'll show you soon.

"Most dinosaurs died off about 65 million years ago during what now is called the Cretaceous-Paleogene Great Extinction caused by a large meteorite hitting the Earth. However, the general ability of smaller reptiles to withstand the hazards of heat, droughts, freezes, and hungry predators allowed many of them to survive that catastrophe and then to exist and evolve even more for millions of years later. Now, many of those older reptiles and their descendants are beginning to disappear as new threats become common and some old ones occur again.

"Let me tell you about the Cape Verde Giant Skink that has not been seen since 1898," she observed, shaking her

head sadly. "Its body was about a foot long and its tail added another foot of length. Extinction of animal species because of commercial uses and human land development that my friends talked about before didn't only afflict birds, insects, seals and sea lions as you probably can guess. This Giant Skink is one of our guests here because it was hunted to extinction for food and also to make 'skink oil' that was used for medical purposes. It may be hard to believe but skink oil also was used by deer hunters to hide their own body odors from the deer they were hunting!"

Passenger Pigeon flew back down and this time she landed on Black Rhinoceros' back. She said she wanted to talk about another of her friends in Our Forever Home. "Geckos are a type of reptile that are popular human icons, but many types of them also have joined the other extinct reptiles now living here. One of our neighbors nearby is the two-foot long Kawekaweau which probably disappeared in the early 1880's. It had been the largest known gecko with a body as thick as a human wrist and was brownish colored with red stripes. It also was called a 'sticky-footed gecko' because of its amazing climbing abilities," she finished.

Lonesome George interjected, "I also know a lot about some kinds of lizards because of my past. Large Land Iguanas became extinct on Santiago Island in the Galapagos Islands sometime after Charles Darwin visited the island in 1835. These reddish-brown 25-pound reptiles lived for 60 to 70 years and grew up to five feet long. They spent their days basking in the sun and burrowed at night to stay warm. Because the islands they lived on generally were dry, they got their water from rain puddles or by eating prickly pear cactus.

"Eventually all those iguanas and their nests were destroyed over time by wild cats, dogs, rats, and pigs brought there accidently or on purpose by humans. But now some of them are back on Santiago Island because the Galapagos Conservancy eliminated the nonnative invasive animals and in 2019, transferred over 1,400 Large Land Iguanas from North Seymour Island to Santiago Island to start the species there again.

"In addition to the Land Iguanas, there are Marine Iguanas in the Galapagos Islands," Lonesome George reminisced. "These iguanas are unique because they are the only reptiles that feed at sea while living on land. They now are considered endangered because of their reduced population, and you unfortunately may meet one here someday even though they have survived for about 10 million years. They have thick two-foot long black bodies with tails up to three feet more, short legs, and sharp spines running the length of their bodies from neck to tail. They can dive up to 100 feet deep and stay underwater to feed for up to an hour.

"What's also interesting," he continued, "Is that these Marine Iguanas have a well-known history with humans. Charles Darwin called their looks 'disgusting' when he first saw them, and an earlier ocean explorer said they were so ugly that none of the sailors on board their ships were willing to eat them even though they weigh up to 25 pounds each. They live in colonies of up to 1,000 iguanas and generally stay on land except to swim and eat in the ocean. They're also unique for another reason: when the males fight over females, they don't bite or scratch each other but only head-butt their competitors."

Dodo laughed and said that it probably was best that Lonesome George never lived in Australia thousands of years ago when some truly fearsome reptiles once lived there. She described one for him. "Long ago, you might have seen the Australian Megalania there; its name translates to 'giant wanderer.' It was an 18-foot long, half-ton monitor lizard that would attack even early lions and kangaroos. It was considered the largest land lizard ever."

She then looked at him, sadly adding, "It is thought that the Megalania died out and ended up here because it could not survive all the hunting by early humans in Australia. Also, due to climate change, most of the animals that it relied on for food became extinct.

"Watch out here as well for the Wonambi," she warned. "It was an 18-foot, hundred-pound constrictor snake that lived in various parts of the world including Australia about two million years ago. It probably was not venomous. It killed early large kangaroos, wallabies, and other mammals by attacking from ambush and squeezing them to death. Then, like other boas, it swallowed them whole if it could. It became extinct in Australia about 50,000 years ago."

She then added with a wink, "One other extinct snake you don't have to watch out for here, because it won't be interested in you, is the Titanoboa. This snake, from South America, fits its name's translation, 'huge boa.' It was about 45 feet long, about the size of two giraffes, and weighed over one ton, about the weight of one giraffe. It lived in swampy forest areas and, despite its size, it probably lived primarily on fish rather than large land animals."

"I'm always interested in the larger animals," Black Rhinoceros responded, "And I heard about some huge crocodiles from Africa. Crocodiles are one type of reptile that nobody forgets or ignores. An ancestor of today's crocodiles was the Sarcosuchus, sometimes called the 'SuperCroc.' It was twice the size of the largest crocodile living today and was the largest crocodile that ever lived.

"This crocodile existed about 100 million years ago, weighed over ten tons, and was up to 40 feet long. You never would forget it if you saw one: its snout was three-fourths of the length of its head, filled with big teeth. Some other interesting facts about it include it never stopped growing over its lifetime, it lived where the Sahara Desert is now, and its body was covered with armored plates. It ate mostly fish but would eat any other flesh it caught."

Dodo looked startled as she suddenly remembered something else. "Speaking of boas, one reptile coincidence I should tell you about involves the Round Island Burrowing Boa. It used to live on the same Indian Ocean island where my Dodo species originally lived. Dodos became extinct several hundred years before that boa did. After the Burrowing Boa became isolated on nearby Round Island because of human settlements on our original island, it still became extinct there after 1996 because of the loss of its habitat caused by invasive goats and rabbits."

Lonesome George was listening to Dodo carefully, but also constantly was glancing around at the grassy ground surrounding them. He looked up and asked her, "I see a lot of birds and lizards everywhere I look while all of you are talking. What about mice and rats and other small rodents? I saw many of them on the islands I came from. Some of them we never liked because they ate our eggs, but others ate only fruit and nuts and didn't bother us. Since they are so small, I assume that they've had many of the same problems as larger animals."

# CHAPTER 11

## *ARE RODENTS FRIENDS OR FOES?*

**AS DODO, PASSENGER PIGEON,** and Black Rhinoceros thought about Lonesome George's last question, their musings were interrupted by a small furry animal with a squeaky voice and a twitching nose. After hiding behind Black Rhinoceros's back foot it jumped forward to join the group. "Hi, Lonesome George, I'm Indefatigable Galapagos Mouse! Before I answer your question, let me tell you a little about myself.

"You may have heard of me back home," she continued. "I lived on Santa Cruz Island in the Galapagos Islands rather than on Pinto Island like you, along with my cousin, Darwin's Galapagos Mouse. Humans' ships brought black rats and feral cats to our island as well. These predators made it hard to stay alive because they hunted us when we were looking for food or shelter and they also brought new diseases that killed many of us. The last of my Darwin's cousins died in the late 1920's, and my species sometime after that, but we were not declared extinct officially until 2000."

Galapagos Mouse enthusiastically nodded her head up and down as she spoke and replied to Lonesome George's question, "You're right, Lonesome George, throughout history many of us smaller mammals have suffered from the same problems and consequences as larger animals. And

since rodents like mice and rats live almost all over the world, extinctions of rodents have been identified in every country and on every continent except Antarctica where there were no native rodents.

"You should know about the Big-Eared Hopping Mouse and what happened to it," she continued. "It looked more like a tiny kangaroo than a mouse and had a bushy tail. Also, as its name implied, it had enormous ears compared to its body size. While it often walked on four legs, it could hop on its back legs when it was hurrying. It lived in Australia and disappeared forever in the mid-1800's. Those mice were particularly sensitive to loss of habitat caused by expanding agriculture, diseases, and becoming prey for cats introduced by humans. In fact, seven types of rodents native to Australia became extinct in recent centuries for these reasons including its close cousin, the Long-Tailed Hopping Mouse."

She looked over at Dodo who nodded at her to go on and then continued with a more serious tone. "The problem of staying alive after humans intrude into an area exists all over the world but it has the most severe impacts when an animal lives only in a very small, specialized home habitat. For example, take the Gull Island Vole which is an animal like a mole. It lived only in the beach grasses of Gull Island in New York many years ago. It disappeared from that island after its habitat was destroyed while soldiers building Fort Michie in 1898 for the Spanish-American War cleared and covered that area.

"I can tell you about another similar American rodent extinction," she continued. "It involved the Goff's Pocket Gopher that lived in just one county in Florida. This gopher lived in burrows it dug with its large claws and ate only underground vegetation. Like other pocket gophers, it had 'pockets' in its cheeks to store food. This gopher generally lived alone and was aggressive only when another animal tried to come into its burrow. It disappeared probably because human development eliminated all of its natural habitats and crushed its burrows.

"A similar end came to another Florida rodent on a small peninsula there. The Chadwick Beach Cotton Mouse was about seven inches long and had cinnamon-colored fur with a pink-white belly. It lived in shoreline forests and sand dunes, built its nests with wild cotton, and probably was lost because of deforestation and being hunted by cats. It was last studied in 1938.

"We also recently said 'adios' to another unique rodent, the Teporingo or Volcano Rabbit," Galapagos Mouse added apologetically. "It was from Mexico and was found only on the volcanoes south and east of Mexico City. It once was known as the world's second smallest rabbit. It lived in small groups in burrows that, despite the Teporingo' s tiny size, stretched up to 15 to 20 feet long. Unlike other rabbits, when the Teporingo Rabbit was threatened by a predator, it didn't thump its feet but instead it squeaked loudly. It disappeared around 2003 due to clearing of forests for agricultural purposes and highway construction as well as due to global warming. Soon afterwards it was declared extinct because it no longer could be found there or anywhere else."

Galapagos Mouse complained that she often became angry because most rodents are not given the respect that they deserve. "I understand that humans consider us pests because we chew on everything from wires to furniture in order to wear down our front incisors, and we steal food whenever we can. You know, you always can identify a rodent as compared to other small mammals because of those constantly growing pairs of large front teeth.

"Also, rodents often are blamed unfairly and erroneously for causing diseases, but that isn't true. We don't cause diseases, but instead we only contribute to their spread because some of us might carry the viruses that cause illnesses such as Hantavirus, Lyme disease or Rocky Mountain Fever outbreaks. It is commonly known that we also carried the inflected fleas that caused the Black Plague in Europe in the 1300's that killed up to 100 million people.

"Nobody ever talks about the other side of the story, the great benefits provided by rodents," she then argued. "We serve many valuable purposes including eating other pests and seeds to eliminate invasive plants, and even pollinating plants. Nobody mentions the lives rodents have saved during frigid winters when humans wore beaver pelts or chinchilla fur to keep warm. Also, as you all know, for hundreds of years rodents have saved millions of lives as subjects for medical or product testing, or as grisly as it sounds, as the means for students to learn hands-on anatomy."

Dodo then smirked at Galapagos Mouse and told her she conveniently forgot to mention another benefit. "As odd as it may seem to some humans, rats in many countries in Southeast Asia and parts of Africa are captured and bred to be eaten as a primary source of protein. The same goes for guinea pigs living in Peru. I understand over 85 species of rodents have been an important source of food in at least 42 societies going back to Roman and Incan times. Also, I don't need to ask how many of you have heard of various rodents being kept as school and household pets. Even better, in parts of India, rats are treated as holy animals!"

"What many people don't know is how long rodents have been around," Galapagos Mouse started again with a boast. "The earliest mouse ancestors were called 'multituberculates,' and they included about 200 species ranging from current mouse-sized all the way up to beaver-sized. All of these early rodents existed for over 160 million years, with one ancestor of those first identified living over 210 million years ago during the Cretaceous Period. They lived with, hid from, or otherwise co-existed with almost every type of prehistoric animal in almost every type of climate.

"Eventually, those early ancestors were replaced by, among other animals, the first real rodents that appeared over 65 million years ago during the Paleocene and before the Great Extinction. Our small size allowed us both to survive and then to thrive during that time and even more so during and after the Great Extinction. That's when they began to fully evolve based on the benefits or detriments of their habitats. Now there are almost 2,300 rodent species around the world," she finished with a flick of her tail and a chirpy laugh.

# CHAPTER 12

## *VELOCIRAPTOR VENTURES IN*

**THE GROUP OF NEW FRIENDS** stopped after walking through the grassy plain and they lingered at the edge of a towering forest thick with trees and sprawling underbrush. Dodo glanced over at Lonesome George who quietly was looking back at where they had just come from. She asked him to tell them what he was thinking about.

Lonesome George answered, "I'm sure that humans aren't the only cause of all extinctions, right? I assume you have large dinosaurs here as well as other animals and insects that both lived and became extinct long before humans ever existed. Are there creatures that couldn't adapt to other changes in their environments?"

As if on cue, with a windy whoosh, a Velociraptor ran up to the group and skidded to a stop. He was a large lizard. He was the height of Dodo and Lonesome George, about three feet tall and six feet long including his tail, and he weighed about 250 pounds. He looked around at all of them but paid special attention to Dodo and Passenger Pigeon standing there. Then he chirped to them, "Good morning, cousins!" After that he turned to Lonesome George and loudly introduced himself in a friendly manner, "Hi new buddy! I'm Velociraptor and I'm one of the older large animals here in Our Forever Home.

"I'll bet you didn't know that Passenger Pigeon and Dodo as well as other modern birds are descendants of dinosaurs like Velociraptors, did you? Even the big frightening Tyrannosaurus Rex is a distant cousin of ours. It's really true about the birds though," he insisted. "Over time, over millions of years in fact, reptiles' scales became feathers and then wings evolved to add to these animals' range of movement for better hunting and self-protection. But before I go on, you should know more about me!

"I lived about 75 million years ago during the Cretaceous Period. Although I look a little like a large lizard, I walk and run only on my hind legs. I also have feathers, three claws on my hands, and a long sharp claw on each of my back feet that I used to catch and tear my prey. Like birds that evolved later, after I laid my eggs I stayed in my nest until the baby Velociraptors hatched.

"One of my special traits that you just saw a little bit of is I can run fast, up to 40 miles an hour, but not for very long. I needed to be able to run fast because I caught my dinner by chasing and then jumping on other animals. After I caught them, while holding tight with my claws, I usually started eating even before the animal was dead! As you can see, I am smaller than the Velociraptors shown in popular humans' movies of your time, and I also didn't hunt in packs like they showed in those movies.

"You're correct, Lonesome George, about non-human causes of extinction often being a significant factor in the survival or disappearance of many prehistoric animals." Velociraptor then explained, "Many dinosaurs, and even more primitive creatures now living here in Our Forever

Home, became extinct long before humans or their ancestors even existed. Why just this morning, I had breakfast with Triceratops and Stegosaurus. Would you like to meet some of these more famous prehistoric animals?"

"Yes, I definitely want to," Lonesome George answered and looked excitedly at Velociraptor, "Especially because I'm probably also distantly related to many of them. I am a reptile, and so were they. I once heard that prehistoric turtles generally survived the extinction disaster that killed all the large dinosaurs. I also heard that a 60-million-year-old, five-and-one-half-foot long turtle shell was discovered in Columbia, South America, not far from my former Galapagos Islands home offshore from Ecuador."

As he finished expressing his excitement, Lonesome George suddenly got a sad look on his face. "Unfortunately, because I move so slowly, I don't know how I can get from where we are now to wherever the dinosaurs are living in Our Forever Home," he sighed. "Since we haven't seen any dinosaurs so far today other than you, they must be far away from here."

"Not a problem!" responded Velociraptor with enthusiasm. "We all know each other because Our Forever Home has shortcuts that the animals living here have used for many years to visit other animals and to show around newcomers like you. These shortcuts are gates like the one you used originally to come in here but smaller. They also make it possible for us to mingle with animals from all the other periods of time rather than only the ones we are already familiar with. If you want a gate to appear, just imagine who you'd like to meet or talk to and concentrate really hard."

Lonesome George tightly scrunched his eyes closed and thought about all the dinosaurs he ever had heard of. He really wanted to meet someone who looked a little like him, but meeting a Triceratops or Stegosaurus also interested him. Nothing happened at first, but then he slowly opened his eyes and squinted. Near him a shimmering gate like the entrance to Our Forever Home suddenly appeared, and Velociraptor was right, it was much smaller and didn't have any signs in front of it.

Velociraptor impatiently waved them all towards the gate. In response to his motion, Black Rhinoceros said he needed to rest his large body and Passenger Pigeon complained that she didn't want to get her feathers dirty again so soon. So only Lonesome George, Dodo, and Galapagos Mouse walked towards the gate and Velociraptor led them through it for their first big adventure of the day.

# CHAPTER 13

## *BRONTOSAURUS ADDS WEIGHT*

**AS LONESOME GEORGE,** Dodo, Galapagos Mouse, and Velociraptor arrived on the other side of the small gate, everything around them suddenly seemed to change. The sun and sky became hazier, the air turned muggy and heavy, and a tall dense forest of large, strange plants, bushes, and trees completely surrounded them. Lonesome George immediately felt like he was in another world. And he was! Through the trees and bushes, he barely could see a grassy meadow surrounded by more tall leafy trees and there also was a tree-covered hill beyond the meadow. With Velociraptor leading the way, they walked towards the meadow to see what he wanted to show them.

As they reached the edge of the forest, Lonesome George began to hear loud clomping and chomping noises and the ground shook under him. He looked over the trees above the meadow he was about to enter and first saw an enormous lizard-like head. Then he saw it was at the end of a very long neck. As his eyes followed down the extended neck, he saw it was attached to a monstrous body with a long tail. The entire body slowly was walking from tree to tree with heavy footsteps that made the ground shake, nibbling and chewing on leaves and branches from the tops of the trees.

"Oh my gosh," Lonesome George exclaimed, "Look at that! I know what that is! I can't believe it! It's a Thunder Lizard!"

"Yes, you're right," the huge animal bellowed from over 40 feet above his head. "I'm Brontosaurus. I weigh about 15 tons, almost the weight of three of the elephants from your time. I'm also about 72 feet long, a quarter of the length of one of your football fields, and my neck alone is 25 feet long, higher than a two-story building.

"Because I'm so big, I have to eat a tremendous amount of food and to do that I must travel up to 25 miles a day while constantly grazing. I'll tell you something else. Most people don't know that even though I look big and clumsy, a large claw on each of my front feet allows me to lift myself up on the bottom of tree trunks to get to the freshest leaves and branches on top.

"I'm not the only dinosaur living here from the Jurassic Period and I'm not even the largest resident in this area," he rumbled on. He told them that the Jurassic Period lasted for 56 million years, starting after the Triassic Period, and was dominated by dinosaurs. He said that is why it commonly is called "the Age of Reptiles." He turned to Lonesome George and offered, "I'd like to introduce you to a few my neighbors here at Our Forever Home.

"If you look over the trees to your left, you will see my relative, Brachiosaurus. For many years it was considered the largest dinosaur ever known to exist. It weighed 60 tons, had a 70-foot long body, stood about 40 feet high, and like me ate only foliage. You easily can tell us apart because its front legs are much longer and its tail is much shorter. In fact, its name translates to 'arm lizard.' To give you another idea of the size of the Brachiosaurus, its skull alone was about 28 inches long, 21 inches high, and 14 inches wide, and it had a 12-inch snout in front as well. We get along fine here unless we're trying to eat from the same tree."

Brontosaurus swung his huge head from left to right and back again, looking for other dinosaurs to show off to the visitors. "I guess you won't see it today, but my other vegetarian friend, Diplodocus, must be grazing somewhere else. It is really huge too, about 80 feet long, standing 24 feet high, and weighing about 16 tons. Its long tail alone had about 80 vertebrae, compared to a human back and neck with just 33 of them. By studying the neck bones of the Diplodocus, and I know it's true from my watching, scientists have determined that it could eat both tree greens up to 11 feet high as well as reaching far down to eat underwater plants. By the way, it's easy for the three of us to get along since we all were from central North America.

"Another grazer that lived after us during the Cretaceous Period about 115 million to 105 million years ago was the Nigersaurus. It was only about 30 feet long with a shorter neck, and weighed only about four tons, like a modern elephant. But it had some physical characteristics that made it different than the rest of us. First, it had a wide snout or muzzle that was even wider than its skull, making its nose look almost like a 'duck-bill.' Also, its mouth had about 500 teeth, almost all of which were near the front, and the teeth were replaced about every 14 days as they wore down. It may have been funny looking, but it was a very efficient ground level grazer.

"A neighbor in this period that you won't see today," Brontosaurus shuddered, "Is the Megalosaurus whose name means 'Great Lizard.' It was a meat-eater that only was about 25 feet long and 12 feet tall and it walked on its hind legs, balanced by its long tail. But its front 'arms' were very powerful and it had a large head and sharp dagger-like teeth. Despite its size, it was a danger to us. It became a well-known creature, and even appeared in one of Charles Dickens' books where it was described as 'waddling like an elephantine lizard.' I wonder how and where Dickens saw one walking?

"There are many more animals for you to see in my time period," Brontosaurus continued. "Many types of fish flourished in the oceans and they included a wide variety of types of ichthyosaurs which I'm sure you'll hear more about later."

Then, looking directly at Lonesome George, he said, "You'll especially be interested in seeing some of your ancient cousins. During the Jurassic Period, there were many types of turtles living in the lakes and rivers. But before we go any further, we also should talk a little about the exciting things that were happening during this time period in the air over us."

# CHAPTER 14

## *PREHISTORIC FLYERS SOAR*

**"I BARELY HAVE STARTED** telling you about the great variety of other prehistoric animals here in this part of Our Forever Home," Brontosaurus' deep voice intoned. "Look up in the sky and you'll see some of Dodo's prehistoric ancestors. The one right over you is a Pterosaur and its Greek name means 'winged lizard.' Pterosaurs existed from the late Triassic Period to the end of the Cretaceous Period, about 228 million to 66 million years ago. Their wings were made of a combination of skin and muscle and they stretched from their front legs to their ankles. Their front legs also had fingers. Different types of Pterosaurs had various types of crests on their heads.

"You probably have heard of Pterodactyls that lived about 150 million years ago. They often are featured in movies or books about the Jurassic Period because of their frightening features. While the earliest species of Pterodactyls were the size of pigeons, they evolved into larger reptilian creatures with wingspans of about three and one-half feet which still is smaller than they appear in movies. They had long, thin, straight heads with about 90 teeth and adult Pterodactyls also had crests on their heads. They were just one kind of Pterosaur.

"Even more threatening to small animals was a different species of Pterosaur, the Quetzalcoatlus," Brontosaurus continued. It lived during the Cretaceous Period between 144 million and 66 million years ago. It had a large body, long legs, and a very long neck. Despite being a reptile, it was able to walk using its two wing tips and back legs or stand upright on its two rear legs."

Brontosaurus then explained why it looked so scary, saying, "When it stood on its rear legs, it was ten feet high at the shoulder, as tall as a giraffe. It could jump and take off flying from the ground, and with its large and pointed beak, it could catch insects and small animals to eat.

"Since some Pterosaurs also could dive and swim, they enjoyed fish as well as land-based food. They didn't have feathers yet, but they did have hair-like fibers to keep themselves warm. By the way, they may not look very large from down here, but bigger Pterosaurs like Quetzalcoatlus had wingspans up to 36 feet from one side to the other and weighed up to 500 pounds. They needed to catch and eat a lot of insects and other food in order to survive!"

As Brontosaurus was explaining all of this, Velociraptor was looking around over their heads and suddenly interrupted him to tell the group to look up behind them at another nearby flying creature. Lonesome George was amazed at the odd creature he glimpsed circling just over their heads.

Velociraptor then explained what it was. "Unlike a Pterosaur or Pterodactyl, which as Brontosaurus said were both reptiles, in modern times the most well-known flying prehistoric animal was the Archaeopteryx. It wasn't a lizard but instead is considered the oldest bird in history although it has many of the characteristics of a dinosaur. It was only about 18 inches long at most, but it had wicked teeth and claws as well as a long tail. The Archaeopteryx also had feathers, unlike the Pterosaur, including some on its legs. It hunted and ate small animals, diving from above and catching them with its claws."

"Now I want to show you and tell you about some of my other grazing friends and about many more of the flying lizards and early birds who live here...," Brontosaurus started to say. But he was interrupted before he could say any more by a small strident voice originating from near his feet.

"Enough of the flyers and leaf nibblers, Bronto! Let's show our guests the dinosaurs everyone always really wants to see. If we don't move on soon, I might take a bite out of your leg!" the voice mocked.

Lonesome George looked around in all directions to see where the taunting voice was coming from, and finally saw a tiny dinosaur, Eoraptor, hidden near his feet and behind a bush, just out of reach.

"Not all dinosaurs were peaceful vegetarians like Bronto and his Brachio buddy or bug eaters like the flyers he's talked about. The dinosaurs in books and movies that humans get excited about are famous because most of us were seriously nasty meat-eating machines," Eoraptor bragged.

"You've probably never heard of me because I'm small and one of the earliest carnivorous dinosaurs ever discovered. I lived about 230 million years ago during the late Triassic Period in an area that now is Argentina, and I became extinct after a million years or so. That's about 70 million years before Bronto existed, and about 150 million years before your friend Velociraptor appeared. The 'Eo' in my name is Greek for 'dawn' in honor of my early evolution.

"I ate both plants and animals," Eoraptor explained further. "Even though I'm small, about three feet long and about 25 pounds, I still could run on my back feet to chase my dinner and use my three claws on each hand and my teeth to tear an animal apart as I ate it.

"Eventually, after millions of years, we Eoraptors evolved into the most famous nasty dinosaur, Tyrannosaurus Rex. So, if you're finally ready to see some really exciting dinosaurs, let's say good-bye to Bronto and move along through those trees to the other side of that hill," he challenged them.

# CHAPTER 15

## *TYRANNOSAURUS REX TERRIFIES*

**AS SOON AS THEY STARTED** slowly climbing up the hill and walking through the immense trees and dense undergrowth growing on it, the group began to hear nearby humongous roars, stomping feet, and crashing branches. They saw an astonishing sight once they arrived at the top of the hill and looked down from the edge of the trees. Facing each other, moving from side to side feinting like they were about to attack each other, and grunting and roaring, were a Triceratops and a Tyrannosaurus Rex.

Eoraptor jumped around also feinting, pretending that he too was about to fight, and called out, "Check that out, folks! Back in the day, about 70 million years ago in North America during the Cretaceous Period, those two dinosaurs fought constantly, almost always to the death. Today, however, since they're the last ones in existence and live here in Our Forever Home, they just pretend to fight for exercise and for old time's sake."

He introduced the first of these two dinosaurs with a full description. "'Triceratops' means 'three-horned face.' That imposing animal had an enormous head on a short thick neck and, in addition to its three horns, it had a long bony fringe or plate over its eyes and across its head. It weighed about 12 tons, about the weight of 14 VW Bugs, and could be ten

feet tall and up to 30 feet long. That was a lot of meat to eat at one time, even for Mr. T-Rex.

"Triceratops ate only vegetation like Bronto back there, so these fights really were only defensive for Triceratops. It could protect itself very well with its three horns and large bony collar. On the other hand, when Mr. T-Rex attacked a Triceratops, that happened because it was very hungry for its dinner! Just between you folks and me, Triceratops has told me that because of its horns and strength, most Triceratops usually survived the attacks and beat and chased away any ravenous Tyrannosaurus Rex.

"And now let's talk about Mr. T-Rex," he raved even more excitedly to Lonesome George. "Although you were born and isolated for most of your life on an island in modern times, you still probably heard about the Tyrannosaurus Rex and that it got its name because it was considered for many years to be the 'king' of the dinosaurs. It grew to be about 50 feet long, was about 23 feet tall, and packed up to 15 tons of muscle and bone.

"In addition to being much larger than Triceratops and most other dinosaurs, Mr. T-Rex could run up to 25 miles an hour on its large hind legs with its body parallel to the ground and used its long tail for balance. It also had an enormous head and jaws with a monstrously strong bite. That biting strength added to the danger of an attack by Mr. T-Rex because its teeth were up to 12 inches long."

Eoraptor smiled proudly and added, "What isn't commonly known is that Mr. T-Rex's size and ferocity weren't his only strengths that made it such a successful hunter and fighter. It also had a tremendous range of vision and could see over three miles away, as compared to only about one mile of sight distance for humans.

"Mr. T-Rex also had a fantastic ability to hear its prey moving and a well-developed sense of smell to know when something tasty was nearby," he continued. "It's not surprising that the Tyrannosaurus Rex often is called the 'perfect killing machine.' Just imagine how some of the other animals felt when in one moment they were peacefully grazing or walking towards a water source for a drink. Then, a moment later, they heard Mr. T-Rex roar, saw it running towards them to attack, and suddenly had to figure out how to avoid becoming dinner in those crushing jaws with their long sharp teeth!"

Eoraptor stopped talking and looked around, licked his lips, and stared directly at Dodo for a moment. "I'm sorry," he apologized, "I'm getting hungry and have to leave you soon to eat my lunch or we might have an accident. I'm supposed to control myself around visitors here in Our Forever Home, but sometimes it's really hard to remember that."

As Eoraptor started to walk away, he turned around and offered to give Lonesome George a longer tour in the future and more information about other well-known Jurassic and Triassic Period dinosaurs. "I promise, next time you're here, I'll take you to another area in this part of Our Forever Home where you can see two other famous dinosaurs who also fought constantly for survival.

"One of these dinosaurs is Stegosaurus which means 'roof lizard' in Greek. It was a four-legged dinosaur with large, tall bony plates running in two rows along its arched back and a tail with four large spikes. It was about 30 feet long and weighed about 12,000 pounds. Like Triceratops, it was a grazer and it had short front legs that helped it reach down for small bushes and other low vegetation. It had a small head compared to its body size and those who have studied its bones believe it had a very small brain.

"Stegosaurus often is shown mistakenly in museums and pictures fighting with a Tyrannosaurus Rex," he continued, "But in fact, Stegosaurus and its real natural enemy, Allosaurus, existed about 150 million years earlier during the Late Jurassic Period, centuries before Mr. T-Rex and Triceratops appeared. I don't know why humans make mistakes like that when they're trying to teach people about prehistoric dinosaurs.

"Allosaurus looked a little like Tyrannosaurus Rex but was only about 30 feet long and weighed only about 4,000 to 5,000 pounds. It also had a smaller head with short horns above its eyes." Eoraptor stopped for a moment to think and then continued, "However, Allosaurus also was a fierce predator. It had three fingers with large claws on each of its front appendages and also had large teeth it used to tear at and kill its prey and then eat it.

"Stegosaurus couldn't move very fast, but it could defend itself well against Allosaurus. It used its large size, the protection of the tall bony plates on its back, and the strong whipping of its tail with its 3-foot long spikes. Modern scientists know that they lived at the same time and fought with each other because they have found Stegosaurus tail spike punctures in Allosaurus bones, and Allosaurus teeth marks on Stegosaurus skeletons."

"Eoraptor, that's all fascinating as part of an introduction to prehistoric times for a newcomer," Dodo laughed, "But you're not telling the whole story about this period to Lonesome George. All we have talked about are the prehistoric animals that lived on land and in the air. Velociraptor, can you slightly change the topic and describe for Lonesome George some of the interesting and frightening animals that lived in the oceans and rivers?"

# CHAPTER 16

## *DENIZENS OF THE DEEP HUNT*

**"OH! ABSOLUTELY I CAN,"** Velociraptor answered. "We shouldn't ignore the really amazing and varied aquatic creatures that lived under water in those early days! Most of them may not be as well-known as the land dinosaurs, but they had just as important an impact as part of the food chain then and also as ancestors of today's marine animals.

"You may not know it," he started, "But all life on Earth began over four billion years ago during the Archean Eon as single-cell tiny organisms in the oceans. Later, the first shell-like creatures called 'Trilobites' appeared about 550 million years ago during the Paleozoic Era, and the first fish showed up about 50 million years later. Most of the earliest fish were jawless and had no fins.

"A good example of these original fish was the Aranaspis that was about six inches long and lived about 450 million years ago. Its head and the front of its body were protected by plates with openings for its eyes and gills. Its mouth had no jaws but had movable plates that acted like lips, allowing it to suck in food which then was not able to escape. It lived on the bottom of the ocean and had a horizontal flat tail that allowed it to swim like a tadpole.

"Here's a little interesting trivia: one of the interesting early jawless fish was the Pituri Shield that had a very long beak-like nose jutting from a long head and long side fins. This fish received its name because Pituri was a hallucinogenic drug used by Australian shamans and the discoverer of the fish thought it was so odd-looking that he believed he might be hallucinating.

"About 420 million years ago, Lonesome George, fish evolved that started to look like ones more familiar to you. They were called 'spiny sharks.' They had jaws and many had teeth, although some were toothless filter-feeders. They also had streamlined bodies, scales that thickened to armor, and strong spines or backbones which connected to their fins, adding to their swimming ability.

"These internal 'spines,' were not external sharp appendages and led to their name. Although these spiny sharks were a big evolutionary step, their bodies still had cartilage rather than bones and were not as strong as bony fish that evolved later. As a result, the spiny sharks couldn't compete with the new bony fish and became extinct about 250 million ago."

Velociraptor smiled and told Lonesome George, "Now we get into the good stuff! While some fish eventually moved to land, the period about 400 million years ago commonly is referred to as 'the Age of Fish' because of the rapid development of a wide variety of types of fish that evolved and lived in oceans, rivers, and lakes. Fish with jaws became predominant over those that were jawless and fish with true bones generally replaced those with only cartilage.

"Fish are harder to visit and talk with here in Our Forever Home because they're under water and don't hear or see us," he added, "But let me tell you about a few special ones that I know about. I've seen the last Giant Water Scorpion called 'Pterygotus.' It was over eight feet long with large pincers and lived during the Silurian Period, about 430 million years ago. It had huge eyes to help see its prey in the water. It would injure its prey by lashing at it with its tail and then catch and hold it in its large pincers before eating it. Pterygotus initially lived in ocean coastal areas but eventually also traveled up rivers into freshwater areas. You might have heard of one of its modern distant relatives that has survived until modern times, the horseshoe crab.

"When in the freshwater areas, Pterygotus sometimes would come across a Rhizodont, a fish the size of today's orca whale. Its mouth of large teeth could slash and kill other fish, prehistoric amphibians, or any other animals which ventured too near in the water."

With a frown, Velociraptor stressed that this was a very dangerous time. He explained, "Rhizodonts and Pterygotus both competed with at least two other dangerous aquatic denizens. One was a three-foot long piranha called 'Megapiranha' that lived in the same waters. Another was the twelve-foot long Hynerias that were coastal aquatic predators with two-inch teeth.

"An interesting fish from that period was the Materpiscis or 'Mother Fish' discovered in Australia. It only was about one foot long and had strong toothy plates instead of teeth to grind its food, likely shellfish. It had two other unique features. First, its fossil was found containing a fossilized preborn fish and umbilical cord, showing that this species gave birth to live fish. Secondly, its full scientific name is *Materpiscis attenboroughi* and it is named after Sir David Attenborough who produced and narrated the 1979 nature series 'Life on Earth' and many other nature films since then.

"The expanding and evolving population of fish came in many sizes and shapes, sometimes mimicking land animals," Velociraptor explained further. "There was a 50-foot long sardine-like fish called 'Pachycormid' that was the largest bony fish ever. It lived during the Middle Jurassic Period and was so big and long that at one time, when its fossilized bones were dug up, they were mistaken by researchers for Stegosaurus bones.

"Another frightening prehistoric fish was the Sabre-Toothed Herring from the late Cretaceous that was almost five feet long with two-inch teeth as well as long front fangs. A different vicious example was the Unicorn Shark named 'Xenacanthus' that lived through the Triassic Period about 200 million years ago. It was up to 5 feet long and had a spike on its back that may have been poisonous like a sting ray's tail."

Dodo interrupted and said, "I want to take you to the next important state of evolution, one that led to all of us being here today. Towards the end of the Age of Fish, these water creatures began to evolve and develop features allowing them to go from water to land. Some grew early versions of arm bones to prop themselves out of water in order to catch prey. Others had hands and fingers, but also had heavy bodies that required them to slither on their stomachs rather than walk like lizards.

"Eventually along came Icthyostega, Greek for 'fish roof' because of the bony cover on its head that also protected its gills. It was about five feet long and had a long tail that it used to propel itself in the water. It had both gills and primitive lungs and had arms that let it drag itself from water but a body that still required slithering like a snake when on land. It eventually was followed by amphibian-like fish and fish-like amphibians.

"A fish variant that was more of a transition between fish and four-legged animals," Dodo concluded, "Was the Tiktaalik. It lived about 375 million years ago and originally was discovered in Arctic Canada. Generally, it was a true fish for most purposes, living in water with scales and gills. But it also had unique features including that its front fins had wrist-like joints and could carry its body. and its rear fins had hip-like joints and also could support its weight. It had a long flat head, a movable neck, and primitive lungs, all unlike conventional fish. All these characteristics taken together lead to the conclusion that this fish lived in shallow areas where it could hunt for food above the water level as well as below."

Eoraptor, who hadn't left yet, grunted and said he was getting bored. He then told Lonesome George that one important fish was being ignored. Of all of the dangerous fish Velociraptor and Dodo had mentioned, as well as many others, none could compare to one that he called, "the Tyrannosaurus of the Deeps."

"You need to stay far away from Dunkleosteus if you go swimming or wading here in Our Forever Home," Eoraptor warned. "This fish was about 20 to 30 feet long and weighed 4 tons. Instead of teeth, it had two pairs of bony plates like guillotine blades in the front of its mouth. With jaws as strong as those of Tyrannosaurus Rex, it would shear cut through any prey it caught. In addition to the terror its size produced, it was a fast swimmer and could open and snap shut its jaws in less than half the time needed to blink an eye. Its only real competitor in the deeps was any other Dunkleosteus. It lived about 400 million years ago and sometimes also is called 'the first king of the beasts.'"

When he finished with his interruption, Eoraptor reminded Velociraptor that he shouldn't forget to tell Lonesome George about the early mammals that had lived both in water and on land. He then smiled, abruptly said goodbye, told them to stay safe and enjoy their visit, and then disappeared into the forest.

# CHAPTER 17

## *SEA LIFE WADES ASHORE*

**"OK, I FINALLY CAN TALK** again without Eoraptor's interruptions," responded Velociraptor. "We almost forgot to mention those other creatures he referred to just before he left. Of course, Lonesome George, in many ways this isn't a completely strange topic for you since you personally already know about seals, sea lions, and dolphins. All we need to do is also to add porpoises, sea otters, manatees, and whales, all of whose ancestors started on land and then evolved into water-based creatures. Many humans even consider polar bears to be marine mammals, counting them among the almost 130 mammals that rely on the ocean to survive.

"Like other land mammals, these marine mammals breathe air with lungs instead of using gills, have fur instead of scales, are warm-blooded, and nurse their young after they are born. In terms of evolutionary timelines, whales became aquatic about 50 million years ago, and various types of seals evolved into water animals beginning about 28 million years ago. But animals other than mammals moved into the water before that too.

"It is important to understand that not everything that lived in the ocean or in a river was a fish or a mammal," he explained. "Just like today when mammals like whales and

dolphins live under water with fish, long ago some reptiles also moved into the oceans and survived. Some of them thrived and had major effects on all other animals.

"I'll first mention one of my favorites, the Mosasaurus, because it had so many unique features. It lived 82 million to 66 million years ago in the Atlantic Ocean and nearby waterways during the Late Cretaceous Period and is unlike any animal today. It was a 40-foot to 60-foot long reptile with a tail ending in a paddle to help it swim. It had powerful jaws with long teeth in a large crocodile-like snout and preyed on fish, birds, and other marine reptiles including turtles for its food. Like marine mammals today, its young were born live in the water and became fully functional quickly. Given its size and ferocity, its primary competition appears to have been limited to other Mosasauruses."

Velociraptor continued to describe those early aquatic migrants. "Another prehistoric water reptile you should know about actually is a real dinosaur but with modifications and it's definitely one you want to avoid. Spinosaurus lived about 100 million years ago, also during the Cretaceous Period. It was even larger than a Tyrannosaurus Rex.

"Spinosaurus' body measured about fifty feet in length and it weighed seven or more tons. It had a large sail on its back, an elongated snout like a crocodile, and a long paddle-like tail. A voracious predator, Spinosaurus lived on the surface of rivers where it hunted for its prey and propelled itself with its tail. Like a crocodile, it also could capture prey on land which is why you have to be careful when you are near a river shore here because our Spinosaurus may flop out on land and try to scare you.

"Over time, one unique type of related animals evolved from land-based reptiles to water-based swimmers," Velociraptor continued. "As a group they were called 'ichthyosaurs' which translates to 'fish lizards.' One of the earliest and smallest of these reptiles was the Cartorhynchus that lived about 248 million years ago during the Triassic Period. It was about a foot long and had a short snout and large flippers. It looked like a cross between a seal and a tadpole and had wrists that let it crawl in and out of the water while it ate shallow water food like snails and shellfish.

"The earliest Ichthyosaurs evolved into larger and more dangerous versions during the later Triassic and earlier Jurassic Periods until they went extinct about 95 million years ago," he added. "They developed pointed snouts like crocodiles and their arms and legs evolved into fins. Eventually over 50 types of ichthyosaurs existed, although all were air-breathing, warm-blooded animals that unlike their reptilian ancestors, gave birth to live young, not eggs."

Dodo interjected at this point, saying that she could finish this story. "After millions of years only two primary types of ichthyosaurs remained, one that looked like dolphins and one that looked like sea serpents. At least one of the serpent-type creatures was almost 70 feet long and by the later Triassic Period, they were the oceans' lead predators. Their fossilized bones were found even in England which raises questions about the nature and origin of the animal supposedly living in Scotland named 'Loch Ness Monster.'

"Eventually, whether because of competition from other aquatic animals including more efficient and competitive types of ichthyosaurs, or for other reasons, the sea serpent version began to die out and eventually became extinct. It ultimately was replaced entirely by the dolphin-like version that could swim and hunt better."

When Velociraptor and Dodo finished telling their stories about these strange aquatic dinosaurs, Lonesome George looked back at the clearing they had visited earlier and then turned to Dodo with another question. He asked, "All of those dinosaurs we've seen and heard about seemed so strong and healthy. Can you explain why they all disappeared?"

# CHAPTER 18

## *A METEOR DECIMATES DINOSAURS*

**AFTER A LONG SIGH,** Dodo nodded her head, exchanged unhappy glances with Velociraptor and Galapagos Mouse, and said she'd explain the historical reasons for their deaths and extinction. "It's all because of the 'Great Extinction' that we mentioned to you before.

"The Great Extinction is what happened when a giant meteorite smashed into the Earth about 66 million years ago at the end of the Cretaceous Period following the Age of Dinosaurs during Triassic and Jurassic Periods. Its impact created the Chicxulub Crater now buried on the Yucatan Peninsula in Mexico with its center offshore to the north. The crater was enormous, about 93 miles wide, almost the area of all of New Jersey. It also was about 12 miles deep, a depth that would hold about 50 Empire State Buildings stacked end-to-end."

She hesitated as she reminded herself about the details of what happened after the meteorite struck and then continued. "When the meteorite hit the Earth, it collided with tremendous force and then exploded and produced even more enormous damage. It triggered a massive tsunami in the ocean. It also caused dust, soot, and hot particles to fly high into the air. At the same time, scientists believe many and massive volcano eruptions began to occur throughout

the world, possibly also caused in part by the collision. All of these physical impacts on the Earth led to an escalating chain of other catastrophes."

"Wow, that really must have been a large and messy series of events!" Lonesome George exclaimed. "I know from my experience in the Galapagos Islands that volcanos can cause a lot of damage because their lava and eruptions, but I can't imagine all the natural disasters you described happening all at one time. Then what happened to cause the extinctions?" he asked.

"Well," Dodo answered, "The meteorite's impact and volcanic eruptions upset the environment of the entire planet. The tsunami caused huge damage every place it went ashore and again when it recoiled back towards Mexico.

At the same time, it seemed like the entire world was on fire. White-hot rocks and other debris that exploded from the meteorite's crater flew up into the atmosphere and then fell back to the ground, igniting grass and trees and burning forests and everything else they touched. Those fires filled the atmosphere with smoke and soot. The volcanic eruptions also filled the atmosphere with smoke, dust, and poisonous gasses. All of this smoke, dust, and poisonous gasses eventually covered the entire world and added to the massive damage caused by the tsunami waves, fires, and lava flows."

Lonesome George looked at Dodo puzzled and asked, "I know that all of that damage is really serious, but how could it kill so many animals? I mean, the world is pretty big, and so were the animals!"

Galapagos Mouse cleared her throat impatiently and instructed Lonesome George that he should think more broadly about both the potential and cumulative consequences of all those events. "Because of all those impacts on the ground and in the atmosphere, most animals not living underwater or underground were killed by the millions due to the flames, the smoke, and the dangerous chemicals in the air. The other effects and damage that occurred because of the giant meteorite's collision and those initial deaths then cascaded through every living thing on Earth," she then began to explain patiently.

"For over six years, the sun couldn't shine through the thick and massive clouds of dust and smoke, killing plant life in the oceans and on the ground. The sky was so dirty it was almost completely dark for the first two years! How much soot and dust surrounded the Earth? Scientists estimate that it weighed over 70 trillion tons. When that amount finally all fell, the blanket it created was equivalent to the amount necessary to cover all the land areas in California with almost one foot of ash!

"Then it became dreadfully cold," she continued, "And the temperatures over the land areas dropped about 90 degrees during the next ten years. The smoke and dust in the air also reduced annual rainfall to less than half of normal. As a result of all of these climate changes, not only were animals killed but the plants that survived the initial fires and lack of sunshine died as well."

"When most plants died and new ones didn't replace them immediately, the survival problems immediately went up the entire food chain," Dodo joined back in to further explain more of the horrific conditions and their consequences. "The loss of the plants and trees that couldn't grow starved the small animals that relied on them and their seeds for food and shelter.

"Then it got worse. The deaths of all those smaller animals began to starve the smaller meat-eating dinosaurs. The loss of plants and trees also starved the larger grazers and browsers like Triceratops that ate vegetation. When they died, that eliminated food for the larger meat-eaters like Tyrannosaurus Rex. After that, the larger meat-eaters that didn't die from the initial fires and atmospheric changes starved and died out as well.

"After a while," she finished, "About three-quarters of all plants and animals on Earth died and became extinct during the Great Extinction including almost all the ground-based dinosaurs. Many scientists believe that very few reptiles, mammals, flying animals, or amphibians weighing more than about 50 pounds survived that catastrophe. In fact, some say that prehistoric birds were the only direct descendants of dinosaurs that survived this catastrophe.

"When humans today ignore or underestimate the impacts of climate change, they should study this history. What happened during the Great Extinction should be a great lesson for what hazards to prevent and what happens when there is severe climate change. Unfortunately, few humans consider an event like this from prehistoric times or its consequences to be relevant to their lives today."

When she finished her explanation, Dodo became quiet and looked around, hoping for someone to change the subject again. Galapagos Mouse then laughed and said to

Lonesome George, "Now that you've seen some of the famous dinosaurs, I'm sure you'll never be able to compare any later extinct animals to the dinosaurs that lived in those prehistoric times!"

As soon as she finished making that statement, a new shimmering small gate suddenly appeared near them. A deep voice growled from the other side of the gate, "Oh yeah? You think there's no comparisons? Come over here, you folks haven't seen anything yet!"

# CHAPTER 19

## *LARGE MAMMALS MULTIPLY*

**LONESOME GEORGE, DODO,** and Galapagos Mouse looked fearfully at each other and then warily stepped through this new gate. When they arrived on the other side, Lonesome George turned his head towards where he thought the voice came from and saw the largest dog he'd ever imagined. It was standing above them on a nearby rock. The dog was a Dire Wolf and it was over three feet tall, over five feet long, and weighed about 150 pounds!

Dire Wolf snarled at them, baring her large white fangs. "Glad to meet you folks! Don't worry about these teeth. Even though I was one of the fiercest meat-eaters in my time, and my Greek name means 'fearsome dog,' I already have eaten my breakfast. I won't need to eat again for a couple more hours. That's enough time to describe myself and take you to meet some of my friends here in this area. Like I said before, you haven't seen anything yet!

"You can see how big and strong I was and yes, in case you wondered, I was the largest dog that ever lived," she smiled smugly as she talked. "I ate only other large animals that my pack members and I caught and killed. We only ate fresh meat from American Horses, Mastodons, Bison, and Camels that lived near us during that time. We didn't eat just anything on the ground, dead or alive, like modern coyotes,

hyenas, and other dogs that you're more familiar with. My strong jaws helped me to grab and hold on to struggling prey, my large sharp teeth could shear them, and my bite force was the strongest of any dog, past or present.

"Dire Wolves lived all over North and South America, starting about 125,000 years ago during the Late Pleistocene, but we're actually much older," she added. "Our canine ancestors go back about 40 million years earlier. About 9,500 years ago, we became extinct for a number of reasons including climate change and competition from smaller and more efficient animals as well as because of early humans. In addition, another extinction period occurred at the same time that killed many of the larger animals that were our primary sources of food."

Dire Wolf continued to lecture as if Lonesome George and his friends were on a tour instead of standing almost alone with this vicious animal in the middle of another strange forest. "You just left the dinosaur area and now you are in an early mammal area. Our Forever Home has several large range areas for early but now-extinct large mammals, what often are called 'megafauna.' They included animals like Woolly Mammoths, Giant Cave Bears, American Lions and Horses, and Giant Apes, all of which once lived in early America. You may be surprised to know it, but horses and lions lived and then became extinct in the Americas long before the current ones were brought there by humans after Europeans arrived."

She then stepped off the rock, took a few steps, and called over to them, "If you'll follow me a little way over there through the trees, you can see some of the other prehistoric mammals of this time period who used to be my dinners or my competitors." As soon as they left the trees and entered a nearby clearing, the first animal she wanted to show them and talk about was so obvious that she didn't even have to point at it.

In the center of the clearing was a huge Woolly Mammoth. It was about the size of African elephants living in Lonesome George's time but had long heavy fur drooping down its sides, explaining its name. It also had enormous curving tusks that were up to 14 feet long and weighed as much as 200 pounds each.

Dire Wolf walked closer to them and quietly told them more about the Woolly Mammoths. "Today's humans know a lot about these animals because whole frozen Wooly Mammoth bodies have been found in Alaska and Siberia. The oldest Woolly Mammoths lived about 400,000 years ago and most disappeared about 10,000 years ago. They not only were meals for predators like me but they also were hunted and killed for their meat by early humans. In addition, humans used their tusks and bones for tools and other purposes.

"Look at its size! A Woolly Mammoth had to eat up to 400 pounds a day of grasses, flowers and shrubs in order to survive," she added. "That meant that they often had to graze for up to 20 hours a day. To help their grazing and digestion of all of this plant food, their molars grew to be almost a foot long and weighed up to four pounds each! By comparison, those molars alone were larger and heavier than many newborn human babies.

"Woolly Mammoths became extinct for several reasons and their size and climate change contributed to that disappearance." Then Dire Wolf curled her lips and snarled, "Of course, over-hunting by early humans clearly was a significant factor in their disappearance.

"Like human hunters in the world you've come from, the early humans didn't just hunt and kill them for food and tools. A number of circular structures constructed by humans entirely of mammoth bones have been discovered by explorers in various parts of the world. One in Russia is about 41 feet wide, is constructed from the bones of over sixty Wooly Mammoths, and is about 25,000 years old. The purposes of these bone structures still is unclear, but they probably were used for living shelters and religious activities."

Pointing one enormous front paw towards a nearby large grove of trees and bamboo, Dire Wolf said, "Look over there where a special local resident now lives. It is a distant ancestor of today's orangutans and apes. It lived at the same time and in the same places as early humans and prehistoric pandas. Please meet Gigantopithecus, whose name means 'giant ape.'

"Be careful when you're near it," she warned. "Gigantopithecus was not a very sociable animal. The one here is over six feet tall and weighs over 600 pounds, but some in its family grew to nine feet tall and weighed over 1,000 pounds. They lived in Southeast Asia and generally ate tree parts and bamboo. Climate change also caused their extinction about 100,000 years ago probably because temperature fluctuations reduced the amounts and kinds of trees and bamboo they needed to survive. Warmer weather killed the trees and the bamboo they ate and replaced them with grasses and similar plants which could not sustain these animals and they couldn't adapt to the new foods."

Dire Wolf then relaxed and bragged, "I could introduce you to many more of the local prehistoric mammals living here such as Cave Bears, Mastodons, Wooly Rhinoceroses, and grazers such as early Zebras. However, most of them stay far away from me either because they were part of my diet or because we competed for the same food."

Then she narrowed her eyes, looked around carefully, and almost meekly suggested, "By now I'm sure you're anxious to meet one of the most ferocious and well-known prehistoric mammals living here. I'm sensing that one probably is nearby right now and is watching us with great interest."

# CHAPTER 20

## *SABER-TOOTHED TIGERS TERRIFY*

**A GIANT CAT-LIKE CREATURE** suddenly appeared behind them from the tall grasses nearby and silently strolled into the group. He stared at them for a moment and then growled, "Sorry, I don't purr. And we probably won't have any other company while we talk. Even today while we all live in Our Forever Home, and as large and strong as many of the animals in my time were, they still get scared and leave or stay away when Saber-Toothed Tiger is in the neighborhood.

"Ironically, my official name is 'Smilodon,' but nobody ever has seen me smile. That scientific name really means 'scalpel tooth.' I'm also sometimes referred to as 'saber-toothed cat' but like I said, I don't purr!"

Saber-Toothed Tiger frowned and hungrily sized up each of the visitors, watching Lonesome George quickly pull his head and feet back into his shell. Then he languidly shook his large head and apologized, "Forgive me, I always get hungry when I see fresh meat. Even after hundreds of thousands of years here in Our Forever Home, although my diet had to change, my instincts haven't. My ancestors and I roamed throughout North and South America from about from two and one-half million years ago during the Pleistocene Epoch until about 500,000 years ago. We

eventually evolved into one of the most efficient killing and eating machines that ever lived after Tyrannosaurus Rex became extinct."

Lonesome George slowly pushed his head back out to the edge of his shell and peered carefully at Saber-Toothed Tiger. He asked softly, "Is that why everyone was so scared of you?"

"That's part of the reason. Let me tell you why everyone was so afraid of me," Saber-Toothed Tiger answered with a large yawn that showed his big teeth to them. "First, I'm about four feet tall and weigh about 750 pounds. That is a really big cat! My mouth can open wider than most cats, and my long teeth are ideal for ripping, both to kill and to eat.

"My 'sabers,' which really are my front canine teeth, are about one foot long and could penetrate the necks of my prey because I could open my mouth so wide and because of my strong bite. My ability to run fast was limited due to my body weight and bone design and so I usually caught my large mammal meals by attacking from ambush rather than by chasing them."

"If you were so powerful, and not oversized like many other animals in your time who required constant feeding, why did you become extinct?" Lonesome George wondered aloud as he continued to stare from the edge of his shell at the sleek large cat standing in front of him.

Saber-Toothed Tiger flicked his tail and sighed, "There were many reasons. One relates to the larger animals I relied on for food. Because we could not chase well, our ambush tactics only worked with larger slow animals, most of which were grazers. But as the climate changed, they all started dying of starvation and left us without enough fresh meat.

"The difficulty in finding living animals to eat also explains why so many Saber-Toothed Tiger bones are found in places like the La Brea Tar Pits in Los Angeles. When animals got stuck in the tar while drinking the water spread on top of the tar, they made a lot of noise struggling to get out or just roaring in terror and frustration. We heard them and then they became easy prey for hungry Saber-Toothed Tigers to kill and eat. Unfortunately, after the Saber-Toothed Tigers went into the tar pits to eat those animals, they often got stuck in the tar themselves and then sank and died before they could get out.

"Even worse," he complained, "Was a severe problem I'm sure you've already heard about. Towards the end of our species' existence, early humans arrived in the Americas and we had to compete with them for food as well as having to protect our own lives because humans hunted us as well as poaching our prey.

"You may not have heard, but starting about 60,000 years ago, and mostly about 10,000 years ago, after humans arrived, almost all very large mammals in North America became extinct. These included every type of American Horses, many types of native Deer and Camels, Giant Beavers, large birds like Condors and Vultures, and various types of Anteaters and Sloths. All these animals were potential meals or were competitors for humans as well as for us.

"If you look behind you, you'll see a dust cloud made by a herd of horses. They were some of my favorite meals, although they were fast and hard to catch. Here is a quick history lesson for you about horses. The earliest horse ancestor was the Eohippus, a dog-sized horse with five toes that lived about 52 million years ago. As horses moved from marshy areas to hard land, and because they needed more speed to evade larger predators, they evolved with longer legs. Also, their middle toe grew and hardened and now is known as a hoof. These changes helped them run faster.

"My meals during my lifetime were the so-called 'modern horse,' although that's a bit misleading because there were several species of horses living in North America during my existence. In case you didn't know it, the early American horses became extinct about 12,000 years ago, most likely because climate change eliminated the grasses they lived on and they were over-hunted by humans. Horses returned to the Americas with the Spanish explorers beginning with Columbus in 1493."

Saber-Toothed Tiger turned and glared at Lonesome George and then hissed, "Because of the question you asked, I'm not sure how much you understand about how serious the human problem was for many kinds of animals. Let me give you another example involving the Elephant Bird, one of my friends from here in Our Forever Home. That bird was from Madagascar, near South Africa in the Indian Ocean. Yes, the human problem was world-wide, even then.

"Elephant Bird lived up to its name. It was an enormous nonflying bird that first appeared on Earth before I became extinct and continued to live in Madagascar until maybe the 1600's. It was the world's largest bird, standing almost 10 feet tall and weighing up to three-fourths of a ton. Although

Elephant Bird could not fly, it was incorrectly written about as Sinbad the Sailor's mythical roc and even mentioned by Marco Polo. What it has told us is that whenever humans came to Madagascar, they hunted Elephant Birds relentlessly, both for their meat and for their eggs, even using their eggshells for bowls. Eventually, there were no more adults to lay eggs, and no more eggs to hatch into baby birds. As a result, goodbye, Elephant Birds!"

Without any warning, Saber-Toothed Tiger stopped talking, stretched out the full length of his body, let out a loud roar, and complained in a loud voice, "Speaking of eggs and eating, now I'm getting hungry! I have to go before we have an accident!"

He pointed with his nose and said, "You can see a gate over there. It will take you back to where you originally came from." Then without saying goodbye or any other further word, he leapt over a fallen tree next to them and disappeared, thrashing through the foliage.

The group moved towards where he had pointed and found several gates instead of just one. Dire Wolf also said goodbye as they arrived there. She explained that she wouldn't go with them through the gate back to where they all started but would watch for them to visit again. She too then ran into the brush and soon they could neither hear nor see her.

Lonesome George started crawling towards the nearest gate, but Dodo told him to stop for a moment. She said she wanted to offer him some other possible opportunities for exploration before returning to the entry gate. "We can go back to where we started through that gate, pointing one wing towards the left gate, or you can learn a little more about the Earth's past and how prehistoric humans lived if we go through the middle gate."

Lonesome George thought for a short moment and then answered eagerly, "I want to explore as much as I can. If I learn more about early humans, maybe I can begin to understand why we are having the problems on Earth today that you've been telling me about and that I saw myself before I died. Why have humans become such a problem? Have they always created havoc with their animal neighbors? And maybe most importantly, is there anything that can be done to stop the human-caused extinctions? Yes, let's go through the middle gate and explore this other place while we're here."

# CHAPTER 21

## *EARLY HUMANS WALK IN*

**THIS TIME, NOBODY GREETED** the small group of animals after they walked through the middle gate and emerged from the lush green home of the prehistoric mammals into another completely different landscape. Lonesome George looked around and saw dry open land, a few scattered skimpy trees, several low hills with cave openings facing them, and piles of branches and scattered bones. He also saw for the first time in Our Forever Home evidence of a human presence. In plain sight were stretched skins drying in the sun, piles of stones, and a tendril of smoke rising from one of the cave openings. "Where are we now?" Lonesome George asked Dodo.

"We're in a special area that we hope will never have any more residents," she answered with a serious look and a grim tone. "Humans and their ancestors have been around for over five million years, although some scientists say that human-type animals split from their ape ancestors 20 million or more years ago. The earliest human ancestors looked like apes, but over time they developed characteristics like walking upright, learning to use tools and fire, and beginning to form social groups."

"Isn't that the same thing that happened to many of the other animals we've seen or talked about?" Lonesome

George questioned. "Cats became different cats, birds became different birds, and turtles became today's tortoises. During their evolutions, all improved in some way to try to avoid the problems that killed their ancestors or to live safer and better."

"Yes, you're right," Galapagos Mouse responded, "But there's another really important difference. Unlike other animals, as pre-human animals and humans evolved to become stronger and more effective physically, they also changed mentally to become smarter, to be able to create and use more tools, and generally to take over the important role of the primary species on Earth.

"In fact, for better or worse," she winced, "The development of those higher level mental characteristics may be the primary source of all our current problems with humans. And that's one reason why this part of Our Forever Home is so special."

Dodo interrupted and added, "Today, we'll probably only see and talk about a only two or three of the more developed types of human animals rather than the dozens of their earliest ape ancestors. But you will have time later to see and learn about all of them through their long history of evolution over millions of years. Many types of early humans and human ancestors spent time on Earth, and they lived at many different times and in many different places. Then you will understand that the "civilized" humans you are familiar with today really have been around for only several thousand years.

"Before you have a chance to see something here soon, let me first tell you a little about the physical characteristics of some of the early humans," she offered. "While most of the original pre-human ape-like ancestors lived in Africa, a later one called 'homo erectus' lived between 1,800,000 to 300,000 years ago before it became extinct.

"This early type of human first appeared in Africa and later migrated north to Europe and Asia. It still looked a little apelike, with a low forehead, no chin, and bony ridges over its eyes. The evidence that these early homo erectus humans left behind indicates that they probably had discovered making fire and made and used several types of primitive tools and weapons.

"A closer relative to today's humans," Dodo continued, "Was the Neanderthal who existed between 400,000 and 40,000 years ago. Its fossilized bones first were discovered in 1856 in a German valley called 'Neander.' Neanderthal man's brain was a little larger than that of today's humans, and he had a bulge behind his head, a receding forehead, and a large jaw with a small chin.

"Neanderthals were short and squat, like other cold weather animals living at the same time, and their bones indicate that they were very strong creatures. They made and used a small variety of primitive tools and weapons and were excellent hunters. However, given the environment they lived in, scientists know now that they lived extremely difficult lives."

Dodo began to look more upset as she added to her narrative about these early humans. "Modern humans are called 'homo sapiens' which ironically translates to 'intelligent man.' This species of early human first seems to have appeared about 190,000 years ago.

"We know that homo sapiens at first lived at the same time as and overlapped with Neanderthals. It is likely that the two types of early humans directly competed for food and warmth in Europe, hunting the same animals and living in the same types of caves. Recent scientific genetic studies of their bones indicate that there were some humans living during that time with the genes of both types of these early humans although we don't know if they mixed with each other voluntarily or after conquest.

"How else do we know now that these different species had children together? Well, at least for non-African humans, more recent genetic testing shows that over 60% of European and East Asian humans have some Neanderthal genes. Often these are the genes that increase the likelihood of getting certain diseases such as Lupus, Type 2 Diabetes, and Crohn's Disease.

"It's generally believed that within 5,000 years after the homo sapiens humans migrated to Europe 45,000 years ago, no Neanderthals were left alive," Dodo continued. "Various theories have been proposed to try to explain why Neanderthals became extinct. They include violence between the two types of early humans, the inability of Neanderthals to survive certain climate changes, and Neanderthals' inadequate ability to compete for living areas with homo sapiens.

"There also is a theory that homo sapiens brought African diseases from Africa to Europe that Neanderthals couldn't adapt to. This is a problem similar to what happened to Aztecs, Incas, Mayans, and American Indians when Europeans first came to the Americas after 1492. Another theory is that Neanderthal males could not father healthy male children with non-Neanderthal women and therefore the race eventually died out."

Galapagos Mouse interrupted to add what she knew about these early humans. "Like other animals, homo sapiens itself then physically and mentally evolved over time with several types of them appearing in different places. The most well-known of these new types were the Cro Magnon humans, named after an area in France with the same name where their fossilized human bones first were discovered.

"Studies of Cro Magnon remains and their caves showed that they made more advanced weapons and tools than Neanderthals had and also used them for a wider variety of different purposes such as making clothes or etching. These weapons and tools also were made from new and different materials such as bones and antlers rather than just wooden sticks and rocks. In addition to those practical physical advances, Cro Magnons began to display a talent for arts, making drums, decorating their bodies, and creating cave paintings.

"As they spread throughout the world, Cro Magnons adapted to their new places, climates, and surroundings by developing new social patterns, different physical characteristics, and useful skills. That's where the trouble started," Galapagos Mouse snapped. "Because of their increasing intelligence, improved tools and weapons, and some instinctual drive, these new humans rapidly became the alpha animal and apex predator wherever they lived."

Dodo turned to Lonesome George and said that she wanted to describe a different way of depicting early human development. "There's another way of explaining early human history that you should understand. It isn't based directly on the physical development of the humans themselves that we just explained, but instead it is based primarily on their mental abilities, technical skills, and social lifestyles. This is the way that most children usually are taught in school today about the evolution of humans.

"During the Pleistocene Epoch, there were three common ages. The first was called the 'Old Stone Age.' It started about 2,500,000 years ago and lasted for a long time, until about 10,000 B.C. During this time, early humans lived in caves or huts, were hunters and gatherers, used basic stone tools, and cooked over fires. As time passed, they improved their skills and created tools like bows and arrows, fishhooks, and other useful items.

"Later, during the Middle Stone Age from about 10,000 B.C. to about 8,000 B.C., humans started using crafted tools including points they made for spears or arrows. Their lifestyles changed too. While many still lived nomadically, others started using agriculture to provide accessible food and that resulted in them establishing temporary or permanent communities.

"Living in groups and in chosen places with permanent shelter provided more protection for themselves and their possessions and also further developed the concept of cooperation. These agricultural settlements also created the first 'population explosion' because humans no longer had to rely only on wild animal meat or the nuts and fruits they stumbled on while hunting.

"Finally, during what is called the 'New Stone Age,' from about 8,000 B.C. to about 3,000 B.C., humans almost completely stopped their hunter-gatherer lifestyle and lived only in established communities, often staying permanently in one place. During that time, they learned to grow more of their own food in regular crops and started to domesticate animals for food, labor, protection, and companionship. They also made great cultural leaps and significantly increased their skills in pottery, weaving, and arts."

Dodo paused for a moment and looked at Lonesome George to be sure he was following her explanation. When she saw he was, she resumed the early human history lesson.

"Following the Stone Age were two other important development periods that expanded the capabilities of humans. The first was the Bronze Age from about 3,000 B.C. to 1,300 B.C. when humans learned to make and use bronze, copper, and tin for tools. They also invented other useful tools such as the wheel and the plow. They continued to develop their arts, built circular homes with central fire pits and high roofs, and began writing. Some human groups, the most well-known of which were the ancient Egyptians, also started to create organized governments and religions.

"The Bronze Age was followed by the Iron Age from about 1,300 B.C. to 900 B.C. when humans learned how to forge iron. This major leap in technology allowed for the mass production of both tools and weapons and the implements produced that way both lasted longer and were stronger. Humans' communities began to have streets and water systems, stronger forts were built for defense, and religious and royal structures provided sources of government leadership."

"OK, OK, enough school!' Lonesome George complained.

"In a minute, Lonesome George," responded Dodo. Before we go on, I want you to put all of what I said in perspective. You've seen pictures of massive boats, rocket ships, airplanes, skyscrapers, and other wonders of human construction, right? None of those would have been possible if humans hadn't learned their metalwork only about three thousand years ago. Why couldn't they also have learned during the same time to protect the Earth's environment?"

"I now have listened to both ways you described early human development and I'm both impressed and distressed at the achievements of humans," Lone George replied. "I also understand that those living in this area are the ancestors of today's humans." Then he snorted, "But that can't be the real reason you consider this area so 'special.' And why don't I see anyone?"

Just as Lonesome George finished complaining about the long introduction, he and the others glimpsed a dark hairy shape slowly moving across the grassy area towards a cave nested deep and high behind some rocks on the side of the nearest hill. Dodo quickly knelt down to the ground and motioned Lonesome George to do the same and to be quiet.

# CHAPTER 22

## *NEANDERTHAL VS. CRO MAGNON*

**THE FIGURE LONESOME GEORGE SAW** walking towards one of the caves looked like it was a hairy naked ape. It moved with an odd gait, shambling across the grassy area, and it walked with short steps as it seemed to be trying to sneak up to the cave. As the figure got closer to him, Lonesome George could see that it was an ape-like man carrying a large rock and looking constantly from side to side. It slowly kept moving forward as if it were stalking some prey.

Behind it, another figure suddenly stepped out from hiding behind the pile of large rocks. It looked more like a human and wore fur around the lower part of its body. It carried a large branch in one hand and started running awkwardly towards the first ape-like man. The second figure quickly began to catch up to the first one and at the same time, both got nearer to the visiting animals.

When they became closer to him, Lonesome George saw for the first time that the branch the second one carried really was a large club. He also could see that the first figure had no idea that he was about to be attacked from behind by the other one. Lonesome George forgot Dodo's warning to stay silent and cried out to his friends, "Can't you stop the human with the club? He's going to kill the other one!"

"Be quiet!" Galapagos Mouse whispered. "Don't worry, we often see something happen like this here. Our Forever Home will take care of it."

Just as she finished her prediction, Lonesome George saw a shimmer in the air appear suddenly between the two figures. The attacking human couldn't stop running forward to avoid it. It ran directly into the shimmering opening and disappeared from sight. At the same time, the first ape-like creature continued slowly walking forward, completely unaware of what had happened behind it.

Another ape-like figure, clearly a female, walked out of the cave at that point. She stopped at the crest of the rocks in front of the smoke plume as she was about to walk down to the ground. When she saw the slowly approaching hairy figure though, she quickly turned around and hurried back into the cave.

Even after the ape-woman fled, the ape-like man with the large rock continued his slow progress closer and closer to the hillside and the cave entry. Suddenly, almost the same thing occurred again. A shimmering hole appeared at the foot of the hill near the front of the cave and when the approaching figure saw it, he stopped. He looked at it for several moments and then turned and moved away to the side of it, giving up his quest and leaving the area.

"What's going on here?" Lonesome George asked quietly. "I thought you said that all the animals got along well in Our Forever Home. Those three early humans sure didn't look at all like they got along with each other," he finished.

"You're right," Dodo rolled her eyes as she answered. "But remember what I said was that almost all the *animals* got along with each other. However, prehistoric ape-like humans and their later relatives were different even though they technically are 'animals' and many are more like apes than today's humans. All the extinct birds, fish, dinosaurs, and mammals and other animals here spent their prior lives attacking others only for food, to protect themselves, or sometimes to get mates. Since they don't need those behaviors anymore when they're living here in Our Forever Home, they don't attack each other.

"These early humans, on the other hand, have continued to follow their older instincts. They often attack other early humans for no other reason than to prove that they're stronger, to show they're better or the best, to steal food or mates, or sometimes just because they're merely upset about something."

Dodo finished answering Lonesome George's question with the obvious conclusion. "That's why we call this part of Our Forever Home 'special.'

"It often is necessary to separate the humans and their ancestors and descendants from each other. Also, none of them have access to these gates we've used to travel around. That protects all the other animals from them. Otherwise, the other animals might be hunted again just for sport or merely to prove human superiority. If that human hunting were allowed, any creature killed here would again become extinct but with no opportunity to come back and exist as the last of its species."

"All of that makes sense, but if those early humans are so hostile towards each other, why doesn't each type of prehistoric human have its own area to live in?" Lonesome

George asked Dodo. "Wouldn't that be easier than having to be prepared break up fights all the time or to take a chance on injuries or deaths?"

"Yes, it would be easier," Dodo replied. "But the residents of Our Forever Home don't think it would be right to completely cage anyone or anything here, especially because each one then would be completely alone without any company. As you have seen, great effort has been made to recreate a familiar environment for each extinct animal so that the living area both is safe and feels comfortable. Otherwise, coming here would seem to be more of a punishment than an ultimate benefit.

"As a result of this design, all the early human types live in one very large open area. Unless they are purposely looking for trouble, they generally never should meet each other. However, when necessary, Our Forever Home has the ability to step in and stop a fight or attack before it starts and before one of last human or pre-human creatures involved is injured or is killed and disappears forever. The same protection exists for the other animals here, but never is needed.

"Unfortunately," she finished, "This type of attack by one or another human creature will happen again somewhere else tomorrow or any other day when two types of early humans find themselves together in area single location. We never know who is going to attack whom, or when, where, or why, only that it surely will happen. You see, it's what usually is called 'human nature.'"

After a moment, Galapagos Mouse smiled and said to Lonesome George, "Well, what do you think? You just had your most serious lesson for the day. We know that this is a lot for you to understand all at once.

"After one more interesting stop, we'll go back to the front gate. We can talk more there about what you've learned today and what, if anything, we can do about the extinction problems in the world outside of Our Forever Home. As you have seen, everything is pretty well under control here."

# CHAPTER 23

## *WHO CAN SURVIVE ICE AGES?*

**THEY TOOK SEVERAL STEPS BACK** towards the forest and then traveled through the second small shimmering gate. When they arrived on the other side of that gate, the group found itself on an ice-covered mountainside in a blinding snowstorm. Frigid strong winds blew against them, and the sky and air around them were almost as dark as night because of the heavy snow.

"Brrr, I'm freezing! Where are we now?" Lonesome George complained with chattering teeth as he quickly and completely scrunched back into his shell.

Dodo jumped up from the snowy ground to stand on Lonesome George's shell and yelled loudly over the sound of the wind as she also shivered, "We'll only stay here for a couple minutes but this will help you understand something else that we've talked about already. We're in the later of one of the major five ice ages that changed the Earth and caused the deaths of millions of its inhabitants repeatedly over hundreds of millions of years during the planet's existence. The ice ages were a type of climate change making it colder rather than warmer and covering much of the world in ice. When this happened, the Earth might have looked from above like a giant snowball. Animals and plants either adapted to survive in this frigid climate or became extinct.

"Ice ages happen," she explained, "When climate change causes the world to cool and solid ice called 'glaciers' stretch from the North Pole to areas further south, and from the South Pole to areas further north. These make the entire world colder. Some ice ages extended from the North Pole as far south as all of North America and Europe, and at least one went all the way to the equator! That is why they had such major worldwide impacts.

"Remember when we saw the wooly mammoth earlier today?" Dodo inquired. "This cold climate is why it was so wooly and large, to protect its body from the cold. It became extinct when it couldn't cope with the later warmer temperatures and the competition from early humans. But there is another unique animal from the ice ages that lives here, and we want you to see it before we leave," she finished.

Galapagos Mouse also climbed up on top of Lonesome George's shell to get off the freezing ice and to try to stay warm. She crouched next to Dodo and said excitedly, "Yes, you have to see this. I'm sure at one time you heard stories about unicorns and then someone told you that those were just fables and rumors and there was no such animal, right? Well, they were wrong and there really was one. Look over to your right!"

Lonesome George pushed his head a little way out of its hole and saw something a few yards away. It was standing still in the falling snow and staring blankly at them. He looked again more carefully and realized it was a large animal that looked like a rhinoceros, but it had only one long horn on top of its head. It was very hairy, larger than any rhinoceros Lonesome George had ever heard of before, and its one horn was enormous.

"Pretty impressive, isn't it?" asked Galapagos Mouse. "It's not a dainty white horse like the legends portray, though."

"This animal was called the Siberian Unicorn because of its one horn and where it lived in Russia. It appeared first about 2,500,000 years ago during the late Pliocene and lived until about 36,000 years ago. It weighed almost 8,000 pounds, about the same as today's African forest elephants, and was fifteen feet long and about six feet tall at the shoulders.

"That size meant it had to eat a lot, and it became extinct because the ice eventually covered and killed the wild grasses it relied on for food. So now you know, at least this Unicorn's disappearance had nothing to do with missing Noah's Ark," she laughed as she finished.

"Many other interesting types of animals lived and adapted or became extinct during the ice ages," Dodo interjected as she hugged herself, "But it's too cold and snowy today to go looking for them and talk about them! One day we want you to see and meet all the varieties of life that were living in what is now Australia back around the time of the ice ages. Australia is special because it became an enormous island separated from the rest of the world many millions of years ago. Animals evolved there that never lived anywhere else on Earth.

"When you have time to see the earlier Australian part of Our Forever Home, you'll meet enormous Kangaroos weighing 500 pounds, early Wombats the size of hippopotamuses, and huge Tapirs as large as horses. You'll also be able to see giant flightless birds, 33-foot long snakes, 20-foot long crocodiles, immense turtles with horned heads and spiked tails, and six-foot long venomous monitor lizards. Scientists still are debating about whether their eventual extinctions happened because of climate warming and Australia drying out, due to the hot weather killing their foods, or because of over-hunting by early human aborigines.

"That's enough about ice ages and animals that were accustomed to the cold," Dodo jumped down and yelled. "This snowstorm is killing me and even my tongue is about to freeze. Let's get out of here and get warm. It's time to go and we need to get back to the main gate before we're all frozen stiff!"

# CHAPTER 24

## *HOW DO HUMANS CAUSE EXTINCTIONS?*

**THE TRIO TURNED AROUND** and hurried back through the gate they just had come from and happily left the raging snowstorm. Without waiting to get warm, they immediately entered the last of the three gates. On the other side they found themselves back in warmth and sunshine near the large front gate of Our Forever Home. They reunited with Passenger Pigeon and Black Rhinoceros who patiently were waiting for them.

Over their heads, the sky and horizon were filled with an array of bright colors as the sun was beginning to set in the west. Wispy clouds floated by, catching the sun's reflection and promising a beautiful sunset. It felt good to be warm again and back with Passenger Pigeon and Black Rhinoceros.

Lonesome George stood still for a time, looked around at his new friends and his surroundings, and thought silently for a few moments. Then he drew a long breath, shook his big head slowly and complained, "I can't decide whether I'm happy or sad about everything I've seen today.

"It's sad that so many wonderful animals, plants, and other living things have become extinct for various reasons over time. Some disappeared from Earth mostly because they couldn't adapt to extreme changes in their environments or climate. But as we've heard, many became extinct because

of the presence and actions of humans and their carelessness about the environment and obsession to hunt various animals for more than food or self-protection.

"On the other hand, I'm happy to see that the last of each extinct creature still is alive here and that there's a place like Our Forever Home where all extinct animals can go and live out their lives in peace and good health. When I was alone at the Galapagos Conservation Center, I never thought I could be happy again or would have many friends to see and talk to. Now I can be safe and contented and I also can make many new friends and learn more about the world.

"Where I came from in the Galapagos Islands," he reminisced, "Some humans are very committed to protecting the Islands' environment for the remaining native animals and plants that live there. They worked hard to reduce threats caused by other humans and to stop humans' importing of new animals and plants that threatened the native animals and plants. These conservationists also worked to preserve the existing habitats and the animals and plants originally from there by prohibiting any more human development and interference."

He stopped talking, glanced again at each of the others, and asked thoughtfully, "I wonder how much of that life-saving activity is being done by humans in the rest of the world?"

"I've been outside recently," Galapagos Mouse answered. Then she shook her head angrily and squeaked, "I can tell you a lot about how few preservation programs there are compared to the number of animals and their habitats that are threatened. I also can comment on how many new extinctions and near extinctions are occurring every day and everywhere. In every part of the world, on every continent, on isolated islands, and in the oceans, we constantly are seeing a growing number of extinctions. They far outnumber the number of humans trying to help them!"

She then was still for a minute, recovering her calm and organizing her thoughts before she resumed, "I recently met the Crescent Nail-Tail Wallaby here. It was a cute rabbit-sized creature from Australia with soft grey fur, a lighter crescent on its shoulder, and stripes on its head. This Wallaby was extremely shy and even here hides if anyone comes near it. Eventually in the 1950's all of these Wallabies died because of extensive land clearing and land development by humans and because of the introduction by humans of dangerous predators.

"An Australian relative of the Crescent Nail-Tail Wallaby, the Toolache Wallaby, had many similar features. It grazed for its plant diet only during the late afternoons and early evenings and was extremely fast, able to outrun all the animals that hunted it including humans' dogs. Despite its low profile, or maybe because of it, it still was over-hunted for export trophies, lost its habitats to human-planted pastures, and then also suffered from other predators. The last one died in captivity in 1939.

"Being isolated on a small island with few humans didn't promise safety either," Black Rhinoceros grumbled and warned. "Let's talk about the Large Flying Foxes on Palau and Samoa. These animals, often also called 'megabats,' had wingspans of almost five feet and could fly over 30 miles at night to find the fruit, flowers, and nectars they lived on.

Like so many other animals we have talked about, they were overhunted for their meat, called 'bushmeat,' and then were displaced and lost their food sources because of deforestation. Eventually, they all died and became extinct.

"Extinction due to human interference also happened to the Falklands Island Wolf that was the only native mammal on the Falklands Islands near Antarctica. A similar thing happened to the Bali Tiger from the Indonesian island of the same name that was hunted to extinction.

"Another particularly typical story is that of the Steller's Sea Cow that lived on the Commodore Islands between Alaska and Russia. This 30-foot long, eight-ton to ten-ton sea mammal had survived millions of years since the Pleistocene Epoch by relocating to the frigid and unpopulated Arctic. It. was prized for its fat and pelts and eventually was hunted into extinction only 30 years after it was first discovered by Arctic explorers. Researchers believe it was the first marine mammal driven into extinction by humans."

Dodo was pacing back and forth with frustration and exclaimed even more angrily. "That's not all! We need to keep talking about everything that has happened to birds too! In the Near East, the Arabian Ostrich, sometimes called the 'Syrian Ostrich,' became extinct around 1966. This ostrich was six to nine feet tall, weighed between 140 and 290 pounds, and could run about 40 miles per hour. It had only two toes, unlike other birds that have four toes, and one of those two toes was a large claw that with one slash could disembowel a human or any natural predator.

"The full history of the Arabian Ostrich goes back to prehistoric times, to the Eocene Epoch, 56 million to 34 million years ago, and its later existence and relationship to humans is well-documented. Its eggs were traded in the Middle East as early as 2000 B.C. It later was used by the Romans for food and even for fighting games in the Coliseum.

"The Arabian Ostrich also is referred to in the Bible, and it became a symbol of wealth to Islamic Arabs. Despite this long and colorful history, after local humans first got guns, and those guns made hunting them just for sport easier, the Arabian Ostrich eventually disappeared from overhunting. Its cousin, the North African Ostrich almost was hunted to extinction by 1838, but fortunately the hunters figured out that they didn't have to kill the birds to obtain their feathers."

"The extinction of another special island pigeon really upsets me," Passenger Pigeon added as she flew around over their heads. "A large two-foot long, fruit-eating bird from Tonga that never even had a common name lived in the Pacific islands for over 60,000 years. It became extinct within a hundred years or so after humans appeared there about 3,000 years ago.

"This bird was the size of a flying duck and could swallow whole fruits like mangos and then drop their seeds to start new trees on other islands. Since there are no other similar large birds with the same habits, the continuation and expansion of these fruit trees on the islands now are threatened. One local researcher who studied this bird's bones said that he guessed it was another human-caused extinction 'because pigeons and doves just plain taste good.'"

"Speaking of Pacific Islands, I just remembered another extinct bird that often is compared to me," Dodo resumed. "The Fiji Giant Ground Pigeon, sometimes known as the 'Viti Levu giant pigeon' was a flightless pigeon that lived on Viti Levu Island in Fiji. It was described as slightly smaller than a Dodo and was the first flightless bird to be discovered on a Pacific island. Its only remains were found with others dated to about 42,000 years ago. While the exact reason for its extinction may never be known, what is known is it occurred sometime after the appearance of humans in those islands."

"You know, we keep talking about birds and mammals and reptiles, but seldom about fish," Passenger Pigeon reminded them. "However, fish also are encountering the same problems as all these other animals.

"Take, as one example, the odd-looking Smooth Handfish from Australia. This fish walked underwater on front fins that looked like hands. It also had a dorsal fin like a large Mohawk haircut, smooth speckled skin, and a duck-like face. It recently was declared extinct officially after decades of accidentally being caught in scallop nets and sometimes, unsuccessfully, tossed back into the ocean.

"In today's military terms, these unnecessary deaths were considered 'collateral damage' for fishing boats. It became the first modern marine bony fish to be declared extinct and fourteen other species of Handfish living nearby are deemed to be critically endangered or have unknown populations."

Galapagos Mouse piped up again, adding, "We have talked about the animal losses in the Far East like China, in Australia, and in North and South America, but Europe is contributing to the extinctions too. Did you ever hear about the Roque Chico de Salmore Giant Lizard in the Canary Islands near Spain? It became extinct after years of collection by humans for scientific research and commercial uses as well as after attacks by cats brought to the island by humans.

"These lizards were about two feet long and had a colorful and interesting mating ritual: instead of fighting, the males would bob their heads up and down and inflate a neck pouch to attract females. Now the last remaining female is living here in Our Forever Home and has no future mate to court her by showing off its sexy moves."

"What is especially painful to consider," Black Rhinoceros interjected as he looked at the others and shuffled his feet, "Is that we mainly are talking about all the animals that are gone already. I'm also really worried about the number and variety of animals that still are alive but are threatened with imminent extinction. The number of animals in this category also keeps growing year after year. We should not be ignoring them!

"Here's a typical but barely publicized example. The part of the world least inhabited by humans is Antarctica, but human-caused threats of extinction are happening there too. The famous King Penguins may be almost completely gone by 2100 because of visiting humans' overfishing of their food sources and because of global warming that we know is caused by humans.

"Even more threatened for the same reasons as well as habitat loss, disease, and disturbance of breeding colonies by human tourists. is the four-foot tall, 50-pound to 100-pound

pound Emperor Penguin. The population of Antarctica's Amsterdam Albatross is down to about 80 adult birds due to habitat loss caused by human importation of ship rats and feral cats as well as being threatened by long-line fishing."

He stomped one huge foot hard in frustration and snarled, "Something has been bothering me since this morning, and I'm finally beginning to understand what it is. We're not seeing the bigger picture!

"We're only talking about individual species of animals here, and not the consequences of the extinction of one animal on other parts of the animal and plant communities. Remember when I told you about the Caribbean Monk Seal Mite that became extinct after all of the Caribbean Monk Seals died? That can't be an isolated example!

"If a pond dries up or is filled in for land development, the plants in that pond are killed. Then the insects that lived on those plants and the fish that hid among them and ate the insects also die. All or some of those plants, insects and fish may be the only remaining examples of their species. After that, the birds and amphibians that rely on those plants, insects or fish for food may not be able to move elsewhere and they too then die of starvation. It's a terrible vicious cycle!

"Here's another example of the cascading effects of extinction. The New Zealand Haast's Eagle was the largest eagle ever known and weighed about 35 pounds. It relied almost entirely on Australia's Moas for its food. When Moas were hunted into extinction by humans, the eagle could not adapt to catch and eat and it too became extinct.

"All of these examples make me want to ask so many questions! How will everything else on Earth change if the planet loses hundreds or thousands of species of animals, insects, and plants in a relatively short period of time? How will it affect humans in the future? What will we do at Our Forever Home if we're overwhelmed every month or week with more and more animals arriving here to live in their final forever home?"

Black Rhinoceros then groaned loudly and sadly and asked, "Can anyone including those of us here do anything about all of these extinctions, the threats of extinctions, and what is causing them, or is it all just hopeless?"

# CHAPTER 25

## *CLIMATE CHANGE INCREASES PERILS*

**"THOSE ARE THE QUESTIONS** I also keep thinking about now that I've heard some of this history," Lonesome George replied as he looked at Black Rhinoceros. "I overheard American tourists visiting the Galapagos Islands talking about exactly the same concerns in the United States. I remember some of their conversations.

"Did you know that in 2019, only 1,300 Grizzly Bears remained alive in the continental United States? Besides being hunted by humans, the global warming crisis reduced their conifer habitats. That eliminated their major food source, whitebark pine nuts.

"On the east side of the United States, native Florida Panthers are one of the most threatened species in the world. They are seriously endangered by illegal hunting, collisions with automobiles, mercury poisoning, and habitat loss that makes them homeless and therefore even more susceptible to survival problems. Only about 70 to 100 of the Florida Panthers still are alive. Other well-known Florida animals endangered for the same reasons include Manatees, Green Turtles, and Everglades and Snail Kites."

Lonesome George paused for a moment and said he remembered other stories he had overheard from various tourists and scientists while at the Conservancy. "Here's

another frightening statistic. Only about 20,000 polar bears still are alive in the Arctic, and the increasing loss of their sea ice due to global warming seriously threatens their survival. Without those ice floes, they can't rest while hunting in the ocean for the seals that are their primary source of food. Also, they often lose their cubs who become exhausted from swimming and then drown on longer search trips.

"Humans share many pictures of these bears floating alone or with their cubs on isolated ice floes, searching for food or trying to rest. It's pathetic that most aren't doing much more than that to stop their suffering and starving except sharing pictures."

"Let's talk about what's happening to whales," Passenger Pigeon spoke up. "Did you know that whales evolved over 50 million years ago from dog-sized animals that lived on land? Then they moved to the ocean where they live today and as we know grew much larger. Today's blue whale is about 100 feet long and weighs about 100 tons. Its heart is the size of a VW Bug and its tongue weighs as much as a small elephant.

"But now, after living safely in the oceans for millions of years, seven out of the thirteen great whale species are endangered or very vulnerable to extinction. This has happened because of industrial practices killing too many whales for commercial purposes, accidents caused by nets and boats, and of course climate change."

"I keep trying to understand humans but still can't figure them out," Galapagos Mouse whined. "With all these animals around them that they say are so pretty, so important, and so lovable, they still do crazy things to hurt them or won't do the right things to help them. Now, many of those same animals are threatened with extinction or are on the way to becoming future neighbors here because of human behaviors that could have been changed."

She flicked her tail with exasperation and added, "Before I arrived here, I heard about what was happening all around the world to all animals that are popular on human social media and pictures. I felt sorry for the American Pica Mouse, Penguins, Leatherback Sea Turtles, Koala Bears, many types of Geckos, Monarch Butterflies and even Corals making up coral reefs. For decades, they all have been adored stars in human nature shows, advertising, children's books, and other popular media. But too little has been done to protect them and now I'm also afraid that many of them soon will be coming to live in Our Forever Home."

"We've been talking only about the extinction problem, but we shouldn't blame only human hunting or land use practices for these terrible consequences," Passenger Pigeon chastised them as she flew around and around over them. "As Velociraptor said, global warming and climate change probably were primary reasons for the downfall of prehistoric dinosaurs and early mammals. But back then those conditions were caused only by nature.

"Now, once again, weather extremes are contributing to poor chances of survival for many living things. Today, throughout the entire world, animals, plants, and even humans are threatened by the dangerous effects of global warming and climate change," she charged. "They all are harmed by the greater numbers and sizes of storms, forest fires, droughts, and other natural catastrophes. But now we understand there is a big difference between the causes of past and the current climate change events."

She then added emphatically, "Climate change in the past happened naturally or was caused by natural cataclysmic events. The climate change problems today mostly are caused by or made worse by humans themselves, either purposefully, negligently, or sometimes accidentally. No matter how or why these problems started or became worse, most humans don't seem willing to take the basic and drastic steps necessary to reduce or eliminate these increasingly serious hazards.

"You know, if humans only would wake up and look around themselves, they would see how bad things already are and how bad they are getting. Then they could save many or all of the inhabitants in today's world including their fellow humans from a new apocalypse or massive extinction event."

"You're right, Passenger Pigeon, I agree that both climate change and global warming causing higher temperatures and ice melt effect everyday life as well as make bad storms and forest fires become worse," Galapagos Mouse responded. "Scientists already have said that human activity over the last 50 years significantly has warmed the planet. They also say in addition that global warming is happening more rapidly every year than it did the prior year.

"These changes have created what has become known as 'the greenhouse effect.' Warming air creates more water vapor in the atmosphere and that prevents excess heat from escaping the Earth's surface. As a result, the air's increased water vapor further warms the air and oceans, creating even more water vapor and therefore more heat. Those accumulated changes make the effects of global warming even more dangerous to all living things.

Galapagos Mouse then said that understanding what scientists have discovered explains more of the reasons for these dangerous conditions. "Did you know that water vapor in the atmosphere is not the only greenhouse gas making the global warming crisis worse?" she continued.

"Carbon dioxide is another kind of greenhouse gas that is produced naturally by the breathing of animals and humans, by humans burning fossil fuels such as coal and oil, and by various effects of urban living. Too much carbon dioxide in the air causes the Earth's atmosphere to trap additional heat and then warm up even more.

"In the past, excess carbon dioxide was absorbed from the air by plants and trees and turned into oxygen that is breathed by most animals. But the overall capacity to produce this change and reduce the level of carbon dioxide has been reduced greatly by the destruction of vegetation and forests throughout the world, especially rainforests. These are replaced by agriculture, stockyards, roads and other paved areas, and buildings, none of which can replace the lost carbon dioxide converters.

"That's not all! Another greenhouse gas, methane, is released into the air both naturally and by wasteful human activity and is even more harmful to the climate. And a fourth dangerous greenhouse gas, nitrous oxide, results from burning, the application of agricultural chemicals, and fossil fuel use.

"In all, these excessive greenhouse gases, sometimes called a 'poisonous soup,' increasingly are produced by or not reduced by human activity," Galapagos Mouse complained. "Without major changes in human behavior, they create conditions that eventually may eliminate all life on Earth including humans themselves. Science has proven that this danger exists, but humans either don't believe it, ignore it, or aren't willing to change their lifestyles."

Black Rhinoceros lumbered back over to join the others and offered his opinion. "It's plain to me!" he blasted with his deep voice. "Soon, we will see all the polar bears, penguins and seals that rely on northern and southern ocean ice disappear.

Then the same things will happen throughout the rest of the world to other animals, insects, and plants like my former African neighbors whose habitats are destroyed by heat, drought, deforestation, and diversion of fresh water.

"Eventually, they will all starve because of loss of food or die because of exposure to unlivable climates. It's a wonder that so many living creatures are still alive! I wonder whether humans can survive mass extinctions of animals and plants, or the climate changes themselves, and how these will impact their lives."

# CHAPTER 26

## *WHY ARE BATS AND BEES DYING?*

**BLACK RHINOCEROS PAUSED** and looked around. after he asked his last question, trying to figure out what he understood and what he didn't understand about all these overlapping problems. He knew he wasn't the smartest one here and had not traveled or visited as much as the others. But he understood most of what they had talked about, that climate change and global warming today were causing many of the conditions that made living difficult or impossible for those animals who rely on specific conditions or reliable access to safe food, water, and shelter.

He grunted in disgust, "We can't stop and deal with only these natural hazards, though, because so many other kinds of bad things are happening that also cause animals and plants to get sick or die.

"We've said many times today that humans' land use changes and development have caused extinctions directly as well as indirectly. We know that our living relatives continue to suffer and die because humans keep eliminating the trees, grasses, and open areas where animals live despite knowing about the bad consequences to the animals. They then replace those natural habitats with buildings, roads, large farms and other human activity that are destructive for all

living things except for humans and maybe Dodo's cockroaches."

"Even more hazards exist that we haven't even started to discuss yet," Galapagos Mouse added. "When we focus on dangerous consequences of temperature change, we ignore the dangers produced by all the human-made pollutants released by humans in the air and water, on the ground, and in our food supplies. Those pollutants also often harm our ability to reproduce new animal and plant generations or just the ability for all of us to live long and healthy lives.

"Let's talk about one of my distant cousins, bats. Over one thousand species of bats live on Earth, and they've been around for fifty million years. They range in size from the huge three-pound Giant Golden-Crowned Flying Fox to the one-inch-long Kitti's Hog-Nosed Bat.

"While bats often are disparaged as 'flying rats,' they also are the only mammals capable of true flying. Even in the dark of night when visibility is poor, most bats can 'see' prey, trees, or other barriers by creating echoes with their squeaks that reflect back to them, a process called 'echolocation.'

"Today, millions of bats all over the world are dying after exposure to what are called 'neonic' pesticides, the most widely used insecticides in the world. These poisons are used on many plants to kill aphids and other insects. And do you know what bats eat? They eat aphids and insects as well as plant blossoms and other small animals that also eat the same poisoned things.

"After ingesting these neurotoxins in their food, bats' nervous systems and echolocation abilities fail and they cannot fly, hunt, or even get home. Then they die from starvation or exposure. Convincing scientific evidence proves that exposure to neonics also leaves them more vulnerable to white-nose disease, a fungus which is another cause of millions of bat deaths."

Passenger Pigeon glided down again, landed next to Lonesome George, and added, "I've heard from other birds that bats aren't the only victims of neonic pesticides. Massive die-offs of birds have occurred in North America during the last fifty years. If you can imagine, eating only one neonic-treated seed is enough to kill some smaller songbirds immediately. Birds, frogs and other amphibians, and even some other small mammals are killed or injured by either direct exposure to these pesticides or by eating insects poisoned because they have eaten neonic toxins."

She then said she wanted to change the subject a little. "You know, today we've barely talked about insects, although there are millions of species of them either still living on Earth or extinct and now living here in Our Forever Home. But several insects that humans like also are suffering massive losses due to agricultural pesticides like neonics, as well as from other causes.

"Here is one example. Many human children grew up watching and enjoying the magical shows made by fireflies flying through the darkening skies during summer evenings. But fireflies now are disappearing rapidly for all the reasons we have talked about. In the future, what will young children watch at night or collect in 'light jars' for their memorable moments?" she asked.

"Another sad example of an insect species threatened by neonics is the ladybug, known in much of the world as a 'ladybird beetle.' Many cultures attribute religious symbolism to these beautiful and beneficial insects that eat pests such as aphids. How many American children never saw one sitting on a flower or their finger without reciting, 'Ladybug, ladybug, fly away home; your house is on fire and your children are gone?' Soon both the ladybug parents and their children will be gone forever."

"Let's not forget the beautiful large orange-and-black Monarch Butterfly," Dodo interjected. "Monarchs migrate annually to and from Mexico and Canada, often flying 22 miles a day. Unfortunately, their numbers have dropped catastrophically because of loss of habitat for their resting places, use of pesticides such as Roundup that destroy their milkweed foods, and climate change.

"The science is clear!! The 2017 Mexican count showed that their numbers had dropped over 80% from the mid-1990's and the 2020 count showed another 53% drop from the prior year; that's a loss of over 90% of the Monarchs in less than 20 years!

"Also, the Western Monarch migrates from all the western states to Northern California and the 2019 count there showed just 29,000 of them, down from 1,200,000 just 20 years before. Many scientists believe that this Monarch species is on the edge of collapse and extinction."

Galapagos Mouse responded by saying he had to get another tragic but important story out in the open. "Did you know that bees are responsible for 84% of pollination by insects of all the fruits, vegetables, and nuts eaten by humans, as well as for making honey? Now they too are being devastated by the poisonous impacts of these terrible neonic insecticides. We've heard that by 2014, bumble bee populations had dropped by almost half in North America, a level considered by researchers to be a 'mass extinction.' And in 2019, U.S. beekeepers estimated that they had lost at least 37% of their honeybee colonies."

She went on to explain a little more about the bee problem. "While poisons aren't the bees' only problem, other human-caused issues also consistently seem to be mentioned. For example, another significant reason for these bee deaths is the loss of many wildflowers whose nectars feed them, often due to human land use and development.

"Another clear human cause of bee deaths is climate change accompanied by weather that is becoming too hot. This temperature rise makes their hive temperatures too warm for reproduction and survival. While some countries have banned the use of neonic pesticides in fields, these other problems may be more difficult to deal with in time to save many bees."

After all of those dire stories, Lonesome George, Dodo, Galapagos Mouse, Black Rhinoceros and Passenger Pigeon all walked around slowly, silently looking at the serene hills surrounding them. Each was trying to think if there was anything they could do themselves to reduce extinctions and to prevent a new rush of guests arriving at Our Forever Home.

A big part of their frustration was they felt that they had no ability from inside Our Forever Home to influence the continuing human failures to take steps outside on Earth to reduce problems such as all this toxic pollution and increasing global warming despite humans' knowledge of the dangerous conditions they had created and maintained.

Adding to this frustration, Lonesome George remembered something else he had heard recently. As he was on his way to Forever Home, he learned that in 2020 the United States government, in response to political pressure from farmers, had reauthorized use of neonics as a pesticide. This approval was granted despite the objections of many scientists and nature advocates who wanted to improve the environment and save insects such as bees. The reapproval was a step that would increase the cascade of insect and animal deaths and possible extinctions.

This action reinforced his growing concern: there seemed to be nothing they could contribute from here in Our Forever Home to slow the pace of extinctions and other unwanted deaths on Earth.

# CHAPTER 27

## *SOME SURVIVE MILLIONS OF YEARS*

**"SOME ANIMALS SEEM TO SURVIVE** forever and I'm not sure why," Galapagos Mouse wondered aloud, trying to think of a path of survival for other animals despite dangerous conditions around them. "We know there are living things in every part of the world that have existed in almost the same form from prehistoric times, through ice ages and other catastrophes, until today. They often are often called 'living fossils.' I wonder what makes them so resilient or is it just luck?" she asked.

"I don't understand what you're talking about," replied Lonesome George, looking at her with surprise, "How can a fossil be living?"

"The animals I'm talking about aren't really 'fossils.' They're just living animals that still are very similar to fossilized versions of their ancestors," she responded. "The animals been around for millions of years and today's version of each of these creatures is substantially the same as its ancestors."

"I know one," interrupted Black Rhinoceros. "The Aardvark is a burrowing animal native to Africa like I am. It has a long pig-like snout, and while it often is confused with an anteater, it really is a separate species. It has existed with little physical change since about the end of the Paleocene

Epoch, about 65 million years ago. An Aardvark can be up to seven feet long, including its tail, and it uses its strong legs and claws to dig burrows to protect itself from the heat. It also digs at night to hunt for ants and termites that it captures with its twelve-inch long sticky tongue and then eats."

Passenger Pigeon squawked, "Don't leave us birds out of this discussion! Pelicans are birds that everyone recognizes because of their large beaks and throat pouches. But almost nobody knows that they have been on Earth for over 30 million years and that they had almost identical beaks and pouches back then. They have the ability to both swim and fly and also are able to glide and soar up to 10,000 feet high or hunt for over 90 miles while in flight.

"The continued presence of Pelicans throughout the ages," she continued, "Is proven in part by written records of their religious significance during much of human history. The Pelican was considered a goddess by ancient Egyptians who associated Pelicans with death and the afterlife. Also, early Jewish law stated that eating a Pelican was not kosher. More recently, Pelicans were held by early Christians to symbolize the Passion of Jesus and the Eucharist because they provide their own blood to their youth when no other food is available."

"A long-time Earth inhabitant and living fossil I always have to watch out for by rivers is the Crocodile," Galapagos Mouse said with a shudder. "We know they're old: they can be traced back to about 55 million years ago during the Eocene Epoch. They are a tropical species, unlike Alligators, and hate cold weather. What they do like, on the other hand, is almost any kind of meat: mammals, birds, fish, other reptiles, and even shellfish. A Crocodile will grow to be between 17 and 23 feet long, depending on its specific species, will weigh up to one ton, and almost always will be more aggressive than its Alligator cousins."

Dodo offered that she too knew about some living fossils. "Many other living fossils are alive today. I've heard about the Red Panda that lives in China and Nepal. It is like a cat but has a long shaggy tail. Its species can be traced back tens of millions of years and it eats bamboo like the better-known black-and-white Giant Panda that it is related to. It also is known as the 'red cat-bear' or 'fire fox.'

"There also is the Okapi from Central Africa, sometimes called a 'Zebra Giraffe.' Its early ancestors first lived about 18 million years ago and it looks more like a deer with striped legs than its closest biological ancestor, the Giraffe. It browses for its food on lower plants and foliage, using its 18-inch tongue to grab and eat leaves. The Okapi's population is limited naturally in part because its pregnancy period is a long 440 to 450 days, after which it gives birth to only one calf each time."

"We shouldn't ignore all the water life, both fish and mammals," Black Rhinoceros suggested. "Lampreys are fish that resemble eels and have ancestors that first appeared in the oceans over 350 million years ago during the early Carboniferous Period. I'm sure you've seen pictures of lampreys. They have no jaws but instead have a toothy, funnel-like sucking mouth. Some are carnivorous and many of those species feed by boring into the flesh of other fish and sucking their blood. Lampreys have long bodies, measuring from five to forty inches in length. After their eggs hatch, the new young lampreys burrow into silt or mud for up to eight years until they mature. Despite their gruesome looks and lifestyle, lampreys have been prized as food through the ages."

"Sharknado!" squealed Galapagos Mouse. "A long-time human favorite fright! Sharks have been traced back over 420 million years to during the Ordovician Period before even dinosaurs walked on Earth. Today over 500 types of sharks live in the water, ranging in size from about six inches to the whale shark which grows to 40 feet long and is considered the largest fish. Sharks constantly lose and replace their teeth, and some lose up to 30,000 teeth during an average lifetime of 20 to 30 years.

"One of these sharks, the Greenland Shark, is particularly interesting. It can grow to be 24 feet long and weigh about 2,500 pounds. But that's not the unique thing about it. It is the longest-living vertebrate on earth and can live to be up to 400 or more years old! These sharks are scavengers, eating anything whether dead or alive, and they cannot begin to reproduce baby sharks until they're over 130 years old. Their own meat is poisonous to humans although, if properly prepared and dried for at least four months, it merely is intoxicating because of a chemical in the flesh to protect the shark against frigid water and deep water pressures.

"Today," Galapagos Mouse added, "All shark species face a new threat. Over 70 million sharks are caught or 'harvested' every year just for their shark fins, and then the definned sharks are thrown back in the ocean to die of suffocation or to become prey for other fish. Although sharks have survived for hundreds of millions of years, one conservation organization has estimated that one-quarter of all shark and ray species are threatened by extinction and 25 of their species are considered critically endangered."

Black Rhinoceros said he knew of several other water animals that are living fossils. "The Hagfish is a slime-producing, eel-like fish can grow up to four feet long and is the only known living animal with a skull but no backbone. It has lived on Earth for over 300 million years.

"Even older sea animal is the Queensland Lungfish that dates back over 380 million years and its ancestors were among the first fish to develop lung-like and limb-like structures, allowing them to live outside of water. The Queensland Lungfish virtually is unchanged from the ones that lived over 100 million years ago."

Galapagos Mouse started jumping up and down excitedly. "I know another one! You forgot one of the most interesting of all of these ancient and current animals, one who fits all of your categories," he squeaked loudly. "The Platypus!

"It lives on land and hunts for its food under water and is only one of five mammals that lay eggs. The Platypus not only is odd-looking, with its duck-like bill, beaver-like tail, and webbed feet, but it is one of the few mammals that has venomous spurs. It has one other really weird characteristic: while its fur looks brown in regular light, it glows with a green color under ultraviolet light, probably so that platypuses can see each other at night.

"And the Platypus has several more very odd traits. It walks like a reptile with legs splayed to the outside, and 'hears' its prey like a dolphin, by interpreting electrical pulses. Its uniqueness is further enhanced by recent studies that show that most of a Platypus' genes are mammalian or reptilian, but it also has genes found only in birds, amphibians, and fish. While the oldest platypus fossils date back to only about 100,000 years ago, a giant platypus relative lived five million to 15 million years ago and another duck-billed fossilized relative lived 60 million years ago."

Dodo snapped, "Well, that's all very interesting, and I'm sure there are a lot more living fossils all of you could describe for Lonesome George. But I also know that the number of living creatures becoming endangered or extinct now each year far exceeds the few who, in spite of the perils around them, have managed to survive for hundreds of thousands or millions of years.

"In spite of these animals surviving for millions of years despite the various hardships we've talked about, it also is true that a number of these living fossils themselves now are in danger of extinction because of the current problems created by humans. But although they have lasted through all those conditions, I don't think that their future survival should be considered any more important than ours were or the other animals currently at risk of extinction."

She then shook herself, flapped her small wings with frustration, and declared to all of them, "You know, this is all really depressing and as we've heard, it seems to be getting worse. I wonder how really bad it could get for all the animals and plants living on Earth today, including the humans, if the climate cannot be controlled."

# CHAPTER 28

## *SIX MASS EXTINCTIONS CREATE HAVOC*

**VELOCIRAPTOR REJOINED THEM.** He trotted over and apologized for eavesdropping on their conversation. He said they had not considered the impacts of some important prehistoric events he knew about. He added that he also believed that despite all the problems the group had identified, they might be underestimating the immediate seriousness of today's overall environmental crisis and probable pending catastrophes.

Velociraptor started by asking, "Did you know that five major plant and animal extinction events already have occurred during living history on Earth? When you talk about how much worse things seem lately, did you know that many scientists believe that the world is at the beginning of a sixth major extinction event that will cause massive extinctions and will threaten humans too ?"

Lonesome George looked at him with surprise and answered, "Dodo told me about how the large dinosaurs all died after the Great Extinction when the large meteorite hit the Earth in Mexico. I didn't know there were other major extinction events or how serious they were."

"Oh yes, there were others and they were very serious," Velociraptor responded. "Each major extinction event in the past erased millions of years of evolutionary progress and

eliminated a major percentage of all living creatures whenever they occurred. They also changed the course of future evolution because the extinct animals and plants were replaced by stronger survivors or different successors that could develop and expand their numbers and variety in the vacuum created by the losses. The sixth predicted extinction event could be the worst yet. But first let me tell you a little about the earlier ones.

"For many years, scientists believed the first mass extinction was the 'Ordovician Mass Extinction' that occurred about 440 million years ago during the Paleozoic Epoch. It really was two major climatic catastrophes. Fossils and geology show that this extinction event was a result of thousands of volcanos spewing carbon dioxide into the air creating global warming and melting the world's ice

"Those changes caused sea levels to rise and many plants and animals died from the bad air and higher water. After that, there was not enough oxygen in the water because so many plants had died. As a result, many aquatic animals also died. Between the two events, over 85% of all species on Earth became extinct.

"Now for a little controversy: a recent theory suggests a previously unknown earlier possible extinction event. The new theory is based on studies estimating the number of asteroids that created the Moon's craters about 800 million years ago. Some scientists now believe about forty to fifty *trillion* tons of asteroid pieces also hit the Earth at the same time, causing a major extinction event because of extreme cold called the 'Cryogenian' that this falling debris caused. Almost the entire Earth became a 'snowball' with icy glaciers up to 6,500 feet deep. While most living things on Earth at that time were only microbes or primitive animals like sponges, this climate change still had to be catastrophic to all living things."

"OK," Lonesome George replied, "So we can assume there were two 'first' extinction events. What happened next?"

"The second commonly accepted mass extinction was called the 'Devonian Mass Extinction.' It occurred during the Devonian Period of the Paleozoic Epoch about 100 million years after the Ordovician Mass Extinction. Scientists argue that significant aquatic extinctions happened then because many ocean plants moved to land, reducing the amount of oxygen available in the oceans for fish to breathe. At the same time or soon thereafter, all the new land plants reduced the carbon dioxide in the air causing lower temperatures which most land animals then in existence could not tolerate.

By the end of this extinction event, over 80% of all living species were eliminated. Some evidence exists for an alternative theory for the cause of this extinction event. Some scientists suggest that all these deaths occurred because of a massive breakdown of the ozone layer around the Earth due to rapidly warming climate, allowing fatal doses of ultraviolet rays throughout the world."

Velociraptor paused to be sure that his friends understood the seriousness of these earlier extinction events and then continued. "The third mass extinction occurred at the end of the Paleozoic Epoch during the Permian Period, about 250 million years ago. Often called 'The Great Dying,' this event was the most serious of all of them with over 96% of sea life and 70% of land life becoming extinct. Scientists assume these enormously catastrophic effects on land and water plants and animals were caused by tremendous volcanic activity in northern Asia that generated immense increases in atmospheric carbon dioxide.

That volcanic activity warmed the oceans killing most sea life. It also heated the land and, combined with sulfide poisoning from the volcanic eruptions, killed much land life. All of these interrelated die-offs on land and in the water triggered additional extinctions for many millions of years.

"The fourth mass extinction occurred over an 18-million-year period towards the end of the Triassic Period. It eliminated 'only' about half of all species. This slow extinction period generally is blamed on volcanic activity and what are now called greenhouse gases in the air that caused major climate change."

Velociraptor looked over at Dodo before he continued. "The one you already told Lonesome George about that was caused by a meteorite strike was fifth mass extinction event. It erased nearly 75% of the dinosaurs and other living things about 66 million years ago at the end of the Cretaceous Period. As you explained, it was not the meteorite strike itself that killed all these animals and plants. Instead, it was the atmospheric and climate changes caused by it and many related volcanic eruptions that directly and indirectly caused their deaths and ultimate extinctions.

"Lonesome George, an important comparison can be made from the horrendous effects of the Permian extinctions I mentioned before. As Galapagos Mouse told you earlier, much of the current global warming and climate change is due to too much carbon dioxide in the air. Today, humans are generating *fourteen* times more carbon dioxide each year than was generated annually by the volcanos during the Permian extinction. While those earlier emissions lasted for hundreds of thousands of years, the growing damage now is immediately more dangerous.

"That brings us to today, 66 million years later," Velociraptor concluded. "Scientists and others believe that the sixth extinction event not only already has started but is rapidly accelerating. While only natural causes were to blame for the first five or six extinction events, today's deteriorating condition of the world's ecosystem is more attributable to humans' unsustainable use and misuse of the world's natural resources.

"Looked at another way, the seven and one-half billion humans on Earth directly or indirectly are causing the extinctions of hundreds of millions or *billions* of mammals, fish, insects, plants and other living things. They are doing this by destroying habitats, spreading diseases, raising livestock, polluting the air and water, overfishing, and ignoring the growing threats of global warming and climate change.

"Just before I rejoined you, I heard Dodo ask how bad the situation is today. One recent study says that there are 515 land vertebrate animal species alone around the world right now that are critically endangered and that each of them has fewer than 1,000 individuals left alive. In the same 515 species, about half have fewer than 250 individuals remaining and therefore are considered at immediate risk of extinction within 20 years.

"Those horrendous numbers just count the vertebrates! Looked at another way, a 2019 United Nations report said that up to 1 million species of all living things are at risk of mass extinction, including 40% of all amphibian species, 33% of corals and about 10% of insect species."

Getting angry and excited, Velociraptor waved his small hands for emphasis. "Let me make one simple comparison for you to show why we should be so concerned. From 1900 to 1999, 543 species became extinct. Normally, that number of extinctions takes about 10,000 years, not just one hundred years!

"It also is important to understand that not only wild animals and plants are affected. This is extremely serious for the human race as well. Why? Because these animals and plants are parts of larger ecosystems that provide food, eliminate oxygen from the air, clean water, control pests, pollinate food, and have roles in virtually every part of human life.

"One researcher I heard about summarized today's problem simply by saying, 'When humanity exterminates populations and species of other creatures, it is sawing off the limb on which it is sitting, destroying working parts of our life-support system.'

"Another scientist was even more graphic, saying that ignoring global warming and climate change is like pulling bricks from a house. He warned, 'If you take one brick out, nothing happens—maybe it just becomes noisier and more humid inside. But if you take too many out, eventually your house will collapse.'

"A third simple but more dire way of describing the seriousness of the problem reminds us that a single extinction can have ripple effects throughout an ecosystem. This concept results in a conclusion 'extinction breeds extinction.'"

Velociraptor looked at Dodo and the other animals and grumbled impatiently. "Dodo, going back to what you said just before I came back, this is not just 'really depressing.' The problem is potentially cataclysmic and is accelerating beyond all recent historical experience. Unfortunately, most humans either don't understand or don't believe that their actions have created this problem and that a sixth extinction threatens all civilization, not just many animals and plants.

"The issue we and they have to consider is whether or not it now is too late to stop a catastrophic sixth extinction and to correct the harm that has been done. The question to ask is whether today's humans have stolen an inheritance of a better life, or any life at all, from all future generations of humans, animals, plants, and all other living things."

# CHAPTER 29

## *CAN EXTINCTIONS BE AVOIDED?*

**"LET'S TRY TO BE** a little more positive," Lonesome George urged. "We know we should not lose hope completely when there's some good news and some good people trying to deal with this problem. Now that I know what Our Forever Home is, I think I understand better about what was going on with the couple of animals I saw on the path just before I arrived here this morning, and also why they didn't come with me to the gate."

Galapagos Mouse looked at him with surprise. "What do you mean you saw two other animals on the path near the gate? Who were they? Where did they go? Did they say anything to you?"

Lonesome George was quiet for a moment, remembering when he arrived earlier that day, and then replied, "Just before I arrived at the gate, I saw a Horned Marsupial Frog and a Black-Footed Ferret on the same path that led me to the entry gate. I didn't understand then why they were there or where they were going. I just saw them but didn't say anything. At the same time, they saw me and didn't speak to me either."

"Where are they now?" Dodo demanded to know. "I didn't see them outside the gate with you when I invited you in!"

"That's right," Lonesome George replied. "That's why there may be some good news to share. When I saw them, they were going in the other direction, away from Our Forever Home. They must have assumed that they were the last of their species, but then found out that others in their species had been found alive. So see, if there's hope for them, then there's hope for some of the other threatened animals or maybe even all of them. There just is no hope for those of us who have arrived here.

"As I said before, while I was at the Galapagos Conservancy for many years," he continued, "I heard about other efforts by humans to try to save animals and prevent extinctions. That is why I think I understand what happened to the two species I encountered on the path outside the gate. Some of these humans' efforts were successful, and some were not successful. Also, many times those making the efforts had to deal with strong opposition from the humans who had caused the animals' problems in the first place and who didn't want to change their ways.

"Listening to the people there, I now realize that I already had heard many discussions about climate change and this extinction problem, much more than I understood at the time. I also heard about various possible solutions to save certain animals and plants because of the work they were doing in the Galapagos Islands and other places to save birds and other animals."

Lonesome George thought for a moment and then continued, "Here's one example. In 1970, the Galapagos Conservancy started a breeding program for the last 15 remaining giant Espanola Island Tortoises. During the next

50 years of captive breeding, staff and volunteers also worked to remove invasive goats from Espanola Island and to restore the island's natural ecological systems. Recently, almost 1,900 young tortoises and the original 15 old breeding tortoises were returned to the island to live in safe and supportive conditions as they did before human-caused problems decimated their population.

"Even though I didn't have the opportunity to do the same thing because they never found a living female from my species, I'm glad those Espanola Island Tortoises found a great way to begin their retirement!"

Lonesome George then beamed and added, "Here's another important partial solution to global warming that's happening. People talked about important conservation efforts for the Amazon Rainforest in eight South American countries including Ecuador, Peru, and Brazil. International governments, private environmental organizations, and others are fighting back against the intentional burning of the dense tropical rainforests there. The trees and brush in these rainforests are being burnt down only to create more or larger private farms and stockyards.

"What the local business farmers don't understand is that these rainforests are not only homes for many animals, insects, and plants that already are rare and are in greater danger of extinction. They also are homes for indigenous humans scattered in small hidden tribes who have lived there for centuries.

The rainforest burning also creates a dangerous lose-lose environmental situation. On one hand, the burnt trees in the tropical rainforests no longer absorb or soak up some of the two billion tons of carbon dioxide necessary to reduce global warming. On the other hand, unfortunately, burning these trees adds even more particles and carbon dioxide to the air. Both of these consequences add to the causes and consequences of global warming."

"Speaking of preserving habitats," Galapagos Mouse asked, "Did you know that over three-fourths of the Earth's land area already has been altered by humans, and that in most parts of the world, less than 10% of the land areas remain undeveloped? This massive amount of human land development is a primary reason for loss of habitat and consequently the extinction or threatened extinction of many species of animals and plants.

"In 2010, the United Nations proposed that all nations set aside at least 17% of their land to preserve the diversity of wildlife in protected ecosystems. Called the 'Aichi Biodiversity Targets,' this goal was adopted by 190 countries, but the United States refused to sign. Now, a 2020 proposed United Nations agreement establishes a target of 30% of both the world's land and oceans for preservation. Unfortunately, that target may be both too late and too little for hundreds or thousands of the world's living things.

"And that's not the only big plan we've heard about." Galapagos Mouse continued. "An international conservation organization has announced a campaign called 'New Deal for Nature and People.' Its goal is to protect and restore nature for both people and the planet by completely stopping destruction of habits and extinctions and by cutting in half the negative environmental impacts of global human production and consumption. Its supporters will work with government leaders, the United Nations Biodiversity Convention, and both private and public sectors of the world to provide enough safe food and water for the world's population, create a stable environment, and prevent mass extinctions. We only can hope that these big plans can be translated into effective action!"

Lonesome George vigorously started nodding his head excitedly as he remembered more news he had overheard. "Worldwide efforts aren't the only ones we should talk about as cures, since even small individual countries can have a big impact and then set good examples for other countries."

He then explained that Costa Rica has less than one-third of one percent of the Earth's surface but has over six percent of the world's animal and plant diversity. That country's national government set aside 25 percent of all the country's land for nature preserves and national parks. As a result, a wide variety of unique plants and animals there are able to live safely in those protected areas without fear of intrusion by agricultural or urban development. They also are free from pesticides and other harmful human behavior.

"There also is an important secondary benefit to the country and the people living there. These preserves encourage "eco-tourism" for people to come to learn about and enjoy nature and the rich diversity of Costa Rica's animals and plants.

"Even in Asia where very limited attention has been paid to environmental problems due to poverty and other issues, some existing threats finally are being addressed," Lonesome George added. "I learned that in just the last 30 years, the Sumatran Elephants and the Sumatran Orangutans lost 70%

of their habitats in the old growth forests that were being torn down or burnt. These losses occurred with government and corporate support because farmers and the government wanted to develop tree plantations to be used for palm oil production for cookies and cosmetics and for paper, as well as to plant other types of commercial products.

"Now, many people and organizations there and elsewhere in the world have begun to take steps to try to stop that spread of agriculture and to save the remaining jungles and the many animals living in them. This movement happened because those particular animals were identified and their plight graphically described. That publicity led to them being declared as 'critically endangered' and people wanted to save them if it weren't too late."

"I know about another creative program for preventing extinctions of some endangered animals that we haven't talked about yet," Passenger Pigeon chimed in. "As much as I hated being caged alone during my life in the Cincinnati Zoo, many zoos now actively are doing more than just displaying rare and common animals for children and their parents to look at.

"Today, about 230 zoos and aquariums in the United States accredited by the Association of Zoos and Aquariums have programs called the 'Species Survival Plan Program' and 'SAFE: Saving Animals From Extinction.' Zoo and aquarium programs like these support conservation efforts and oversee the breeding of certain endangered or threatened animals to restart those species or to help create healthy and self-sustaining populations that are stable.

"The ultimate goal of these animal programs is to someday reintroduce captive-raised endangered species back into their native wild habitats," she added, "But only when it is safe to do so. Animal species always benefit when humans pay attention to preventing and eliminating threats to survival and these conservation programs already have helped prevent the final extinctions of California Condors, Red Wolves, American Bald Eagles, and a number of other critically rare animals that once again are living in the wild."

Passenger Pigeon looked around at the others and asked, "Are humans beginning to wake up to the problem? Anyone know of other beneficial programs?"

# CHAPTER 30

## *GORILLAS, OTHERS GET PROTECTIONS*

**"THERE ALSO ARE MANY OTHER** good news and some bad news stories that we can share," Lonesome George added excitedly. "The United States and some other countries have many laws requiring environmental reviews and proposals for eliminating or reducing environmental hazards before certain human activities such as land development that might harm the environment can take place. They also have laws requiring the listing of endangered and threatened species and requiring protections for them. All these laws help protect animals and other endangered living things by making them subject to special care and attention.

"Unfortunately," he complained, "Many of these laws still are ignored or misused. This happens because of political pressures that favor the development rights of some powerful humans and corporations that can outweigh the safety and preservation of the animals and plants and their habitats. But the good news is that some humans and environmental advocacy organizations are beginning to fight back by filing lawsuits and supporting individual and group actions to force compliance and protection. Public promises to support conservation and to reverse climate change and

global warming also have become issues discussed in many political campaigns for city, state, and federal positions."

Dodo glared at Lonesome George and grumbled, "My Debbie Downer is showing again! I don't know how you can be so optimistic when things are going so badly overall. The latest report of the international Living Planet Index is just horrifying.

"This Index tracks almost 21,000 populations of 4,392 species around the world. It just announced that the Index shows an average 68% decrease in population sizes of mammals, birds, reptiles, amphibians, and fish between 1970 and 2016. The primary cause of these losses is changes in land and sea use, including habitat loss and degradation, and other causes are species overexploitation, invasive species and disease, pollution, and climate change.

"Of particular concern to what we've been talking about, that report adds that global climate change is projected to become as or more important than those other causes of population decreases in the coming decades. In fact it already is extremely serious in Africa, Latin America, and the Caribbean. What can a few lawsuits in the United States do if most people don't give a darn about the growing environmental problems around the rest of the world?"

Black Rhinoceros told Dodo to calm down and said that he was once told, when confronted with numerous interrelated problems and was looking for solutions, that any journey is made up of individual steps. And to prove that, he wanted to offer a different viewpoint. "Before I arrived here, I also heard about some hopeful human activities in Africa to deal with a different problem more directly effecting rhinoceroses and many other animals living there. Countries throughout the world finally are taking steps to stop illegal poaching of endangered animals in Africa.

"This illegal hunting has destroyed most of the existing populations of Rhinoceroses, Elephants, Gorillas, and Pangolins, among other wild animals. Usually they were being killed only for their pelts, horns, bones, scales, and internal organs. Then the rest of their bodies were left to rot or be eaten by other animals and insects. The poachers never considered the animals' continued importance as part of the overall life cycle and ecosystem in Africa. I just hope that those new protections are a permanent step in the right direction and are not too little, too late!

"Speaking of gorillas," he continued, "Do you know about Eastern Africa's Mountain Gorillas? Historically, their ancestors have existed since about the Oligocene Epoch about 34 million to 24 million years ago, and gorillas split from their common ancestor with humans and chimpanzees about nine million years ago. The Mountain Gorilla males weigh about 400 pounds, are about six feet tall, and live together in long-term family groups. In 2008, only about 650 of these gorillas still were alive, but recently their population has grown to about 1,000 because of special programs protecting them. Of course, they still are greatly endangered.

"These Mountain Gorillas have been saved so far because Rwanda and nearby counties have established preserves to protect them by reducing the spread of farming, tree harvesting, and village expansions. They also have banned poaching with some success. To reduce the impact on local humans, several international organizations have established programs in those countries to provide alternate sources of food and income for local residents who needed new sources of family support rather than farming or hunting.

"Unfortunately, some poaching still occurs and some of the preserves even are being reduced for expansion of agriculture and livestock grazing. How will they be doing in 20 or 50 years? I don't know but I can hope that an East African Mountain Gorilla never has to join us here in Our Forever Home."

"Come on, folks," countered Dodo, "That's just one of maybe a few programs working in the right direction. If we're still beginning to see more extinct animals arriving weekly, how could things be getting better?" What Dodo didn't know was that more positive things were happening in the world that she and the others didn't know about yet and that undercut her pessimism. They generally fell into two categories, species saved and species rediscovered.

On March 3, 2020, known as World Wildlife Day, scientists, environmentalists, and animal activists celebrated victories for themselves, natural habitats, and some special animals that had been saved from extinction. After over two million Humpback Whales were killed in the 1800's through mid-1900's, they had been on the brink of extinction. Then, after global trade in whale products was banned and limits were placed on continued whaling, their populations bounced back tremendously.

They also celebrated several other saved species of animals. In the mid-1960's, only 487 breeding pairs of American Bald Eagles remained alive; but after DDT was identified as the culprit and banned, and protections under the Endangered Species Act were imposed, they also recovered and even came off the threatened species list in 2007. Other endangered animals seeing major population rebounds in recent years included Indian Tigers, American Brown Pelicans, North American Gray Wolves—that increased from about 300 to 5,443—and Steller Sea Lions.

Even more hopeful but less commonly known are the serendipitous rediscoveries of animals assumed to have been extinct, sometimes called "Lazarus creatures." The Somali Elephant Shrew, known for its long nose, was last seen about 50 years ago, but recently was rediscovered and is thriving. Another long-nosed animal, the Pinocchio Lizard, was first discovered in Ecuador in 1953 and then was never seen again until a population living along an Ecuadorian highway was discovered in 2011.

A different similar example is the recent rediscovery of Madagascar Iguanas that had not been seen for over 100 years and were assumed to be extinct. Their unique life cycle is part of the reason they have not been seen. They live only during the rainy season, hatching their eggs, growing to adults, mating, and then dying, all within a few months' time. But their ability to continue to exist again is threatened by deforestation that eliminates their habitats and by global warming reducing rainfall.

There are more! The 20-inch Terror Skink with its fearful sharp teeth was first discovered in 1872 in New Caledonia but was never seen again until 2003 when it was rediscovered. Another creature with a special face is the Burmese Roof Turtle, a giant Asian turtle with eyes that bug out and a permanent grin on its face. It was believed to be extinct about 20 years ago but when several survivors were found later, they were taken to a conservancy to be bred in safety. Now about 1,000 of these cute smiling turtles have been released in the wilderness of Myanmar.

Many more rediscoveries have occurred for Dodo and her friends to be excited about. The Australian Night Parrot was last seen in 1912 except for a dead one found in 1990; since then, another living one was found in 2013 and its population is being protected.

The Lord Howe Stick Insect, a long skinny insect the size of a hand, was believed to have become extinct in 1920 after all of them on their island were eaten by rats that deserted a sinking ship nearby. However, some recently dead ones were found on a nearby island in the 1960s, and then a living population of 24 of these insects was found in 2001.

The most famous Lazarus creature is the Coelacanth, a six-foot, 200-pound fish with armor-like scales. It is a deep water floating eater with the peculiar characteristic that its young hatch within the mother fish and then are given birth still carrying their external yolk sacs but otherwise fully formed. It was thought to have become extinct at the same time as the dinosaurs 66 million years ago. But it was rediscovered in 1938 near the east coast of Africa and near Indonesia and continues to survive in its native habitat although in extremely small numbers.

In addition to those "rediscoveries," scientists are continually discovering new species of animals and plants for the first time. As just one example, in 2019, scientists with the British Natural History Museum identified over 400 new species. In most cases, these discoveries involved animals and plants that were very small or that lived deep in the ocean or in very remote areas of the planet. In some cases, these discoveries are only fossils of already extinct animals such as a new species of stegosaurus and an eel-like invertebrate that stood upright on the floor of the ocean 435 million years ago and caught food floating by.

In response to Dodo's pessimistic questions, Passenger Pigeon shook her head and said that she agreed with Black Rhinoceros. "I visit many of the newcomers after they arrive here, like I did with Lonesome George, and they tell me that while the big picture of what's going on around the world looks bad, there are many small events and activities that give them hope that the future may be better for former friends or other species they left behind. They say that things could be a lot worse already except for the beginnings of preservation activities to counter extinctions and global warming."

She explained that she recently had heard about one popular form of group reaction sometimes referred to as "consumer activism." "Did you know that environmental and conservation organizations now publish lists of corporations which either help or harm the environment and endangered animals? And when this information is disseminated through traditional and social media, more and more individual humans are rewarding companies taking steps to reduce global warming by buying their products. On the other hand, they are punishing those who contribute to climate change and extinctions by refusing to buy their products or by generating bad publicity about them. These types of activities will have some impacts to reduce the problems we're talking about!"

"But how can individual people think that they can fight massive and well-financed corporations, governments, and other groups who have spent generations and millions of dollars creating the problems around the world today?" retorted Dodo. "What power does a single person really have to counter the actions of powerful individuals and organizations?"

# CHAPTER 31

## *WORLD EFFORTS FIGHT GLOBAL WARMING*

**AS DODO FINISHED ASKING** her depressing question, a small cinnamon-colored bird flew in through the entry gate and screeched, "Hi there! I'm Cryptic Treehunter. I just was declared extinct in Northern Brazil. I heard about Our Forever Home from some other endangered birds, so here I am. What are all of you talking about?"

Dodo introduced herself and the others and then explained what they were discussing. She repeated the question that she had just asked about how and whether one individual can change the direction of world governments and powerful corporations to stop global warming and extinctions.

Cryptic Treehunter stared at her like she was from a different planet and then answered in her loud voice, "Don't you animals get any news here? Even though at least two dozen more animal species became extinct in 2019, people are beginning to wake up, although it's too late for me. Haven't you heard of Greta Thunberg?" she asked. "'People power' to do the right thing and save the planet is coming back into style!"

Almost in unison, the others asked, "Who's Greta Thunberg?" "Greta is the 21st century's environmental Paul Revere! She's a Swedish teenager who is leading a youth

Save the Earth!
Class Assign
Boycott COAL
Greta Rocks!

movement around the world for environmental protection and against global warming," Cryptic Treehunter answered. "She formed 'Fridays for Future' to sponsor weekly student school strikes. She sailed across the Atlantic Ocean instead of flying in order to show how to reduce carbon emissions while traveling.

"Greta also has spoken in person to the United States Congress and the United Nations. When she spoke in 2019 to a large group of important government and business leaders in Davos, Switzerland, what everyone remembered was her urgent warning to them. She told them, 'I want you to act as if your house is on fire, because it is!'

"She's so famous and effective about expressing herself about climate change and providing leadership to reverse it that she has been nominated twice for the Nobel Peace Prize and was Time Magazine's 'Person of the Year' for 2019. She has been invited to speak to world business leaders, religious leaders, other government agencies, and environmental organizations.

"Greta now is leading climate protests throughout the world. She's waking up young people about the environment like never before by vociferously holding the current generations of adults responsible for global warning and arousing young people to take the lead to save the world. And in answer to your question, Dodo, Greta is just one person and not only that, she's only a teenager!"

Cryptic Treehunter jumped around excitedly and continued extolling the Swedish teenager. "Greta has a simple and clear answer when government leaders and large corporations throughout the world ignore the alarm she and her followers are raising. When that happens, she tells young climate change activists to adopt the tools of older social and political activists when they fought for civil rights, against unjust wars, for voting rights, and in other popular social movements. What these young people are doing and beginning to achieve is hard to believe!

"They are holding student walk-outs and sit-ins. They are educating the public to boycott companies that excessively pollute or contribute to deforestation in order to force them to change their corporate decisions. They also directly urge companies and individuals to become carbon-neutral by incorporating sustainable energy products such as solar electricity to reduce pollution, and to reduce their carbon footprints by ending their use of polluting materials like coal and fossil fuels.

"In the United States, she and her cohorts support Native American water protectors as well as Latinx communities and other marginalized groups seeking broad environmental justice goals where they live and work in order to achieve safer homes, schools and working conditions.

"There is no question, just before I had to come here to Our Forever Home, that this environmental and conservation activism movement is getting increasing attention and growing daily! And Dodo, I'll remind you again in case you forgot already: she's just one teenage girl!" Cryptic Treehunter finished.

All of them also were not aware of another major event because of their being isolated in Our Forever Home. The year 2020 was the 50th anniversary celebration of Earth Day, the world's largest civic environmental event. During that

Earth Day celebration millions of people around the world participated in many activities such as advocacy and education programs demonstrating the harmful impacts of climate change and how to try to slow or eliminate its causes.

The celebration also included a massive "Global Cleanup" to clear trash from rivers, beaches, and nature trails. Advocates met to design the beginning or expansion of scientific initiatives to both slow and reverse global warming. Even though it would take years if not decades to see whether or not these initiatives and actions would be successful, just starting momentum gave the participants hope for the future.

Although they didn't know about all of this most recent animal and environmental protection activism, what Lonesome George and his friends learned from their own past experiences and their earlier talks during the day, as well as from Cryptic Treehunter, was that progress to reverse the accelerating extinctions and global warming or climate change still was possible.

They began to believe that more humans than they previously knew about now cared and were starting to take more action to help reverse these crises. As a result, increasing numbers of threatened creatures and their habitats might be saved if even more humans adopted these goals.

The six animals standing there now looked at each other and finally smiled a little. Maybe, they each thought, there still was realistic hope to stem the tide of extinctions and new arrivals. They still wished, though, that there was something they could do more directly from inside Our Forever Home to have an influence on humans outside on Earth.

Suddenly, as if a giant unseen and silent alarm had been triggered inside Our Forever Home, a cacophony of loud and repeated roars, barking, whining, chattering, wings flapping, feet stomping, water splashing, and other myriad noises and movement arose around them, instantly jarring their new sense of optimism and happiness. What was happening? What was wrong in Our Forever Home?

# CHAPTER 32

## *CAN HUMANS SAVE THE EARTH?*

**LONESOME GEORGE** and his new friends standing by the main entry gate were startled by all these loud noises and confusing activity, and they all throned and looked behind themselves into Our Forever Home. They saw a horde of other animals running, flying, and crawling towards them and looking or gesturing towards the entry gate. They also could see the water in the river splashing and foaming because of the excited thrashing of fish and other animals living there.

When they turned back around and looked through the gate to see what all the animals were so excited about, they were astonished at what they saw. There, on the dirt path outside the gate, they could see a human man and human woman wearing dirty tattered clothing, old shoes, and backpacks painfully and slowly limping towards them.

The two gaunt and dirty humans stopped outside the gate and tiredly looked at the animals inside the gate. Then both humans began to plead to be let into Our Forever Home. The man begged, "Please give us sanctuary. The entire world is threatened by war, poverty, famine, global warming, and incurable epidemics. Our cities and countrysides are being destroyed by floods, fires, rising oceans, hurricanes and tornados, other natural disasters, and man-made toxic

catastrophes. People everywhere are dying, starving, sick, helpless, and hopeless. And it's only going to get worse. We need safe shelter so that humanity can survive."

With tears in her eyes, the woman also pleaded, "We're not selfishly only trying to save ourselves! We only want an opportunity to do what we can to make a new start for the human race. After that, when we return outside with our new families and friends, we will do a better job taking care of the planet.

"We know because of our knowledge of the past mistakes we and others have made what we must do to avoid making them again. We can help create and then maintain a new healthy and just society and world for all people. We know we can do this! Please, please, let us in, save us and give us a chance!"

Dodo looked back again at all the animals surrounding her and her friends. They now were calmer and quieter but still anxiously milling around and listening to every word. She also looked longingly past them at the beautiful and serene hills, rivers, plants, and trees of Our Forever Home. She thought for a while about what the humans had said before responding to the couple's requests.

After a few moments Dodo said quietly, "You need to understand one important thing: what those of us who live here are most afraid of is not what you are reporting about today's conditions around the Earth. We all are the proof of what all those conditions have created in the past and that they have been getting worse again. Instead, what we fear most is that you are humans and that you want to 'start over again.'"

She looked at the couple disapprovingly. "When you explained why you wanted to come into Our Forever Home, you didn't mention or include all the harm happening to any of Earth's living things other than you humans. You didn't talk about the thousands of species of plants and animals that have become endangered and extinct in recent years because of your actions and inactions and what might happen to those still living.

"When you described your predicament and asked for help, you also didn't say that your goal includes preserving and protecting animals such as ourselves, plants, and the rest of the living environment. You only talked about humans.

"To those of us living here, that is not at all at all surprising. Through millions of years, our experience is that most of you humans think only of your own needs, desires, amusement, and profits, and little else on Earth seems to stand in the way of achieving those goals or otherwise matter.

"That selfish way of thinking is a primary reason for both the unhealthy and dangerous conditions now existing on Earth and the current steadily increasing population of Our Forever Home. Extinctions and extreme population loss of all types of living things on Earth are increasing even though humans have the technology, ability, and knowledge to reverse those trends," Dodo continued indignantly with a dark frown. "And taking all of this into consideration, I'm not sure that even now you have learned or understand what needs to be learned or understood."

She glared angrily at them for a long time, shook her head, and then turned to look questioningly at her six friends and the other animals surrounding them. After seeing the faces of all those animals, she turned back to the two humans and shook her head dismissively.

The humans were stunned. The man's shoulders slumped as he began to realize that their request might be refused. The woman just continued to stare into Our Forever Home. She then weakly smiled at her partner and exclaimed, "Look! Can you see inside? There are butterflies flitting around. The sky is blue instead of hazy and dark. And look at all the birds and streams and the gorgeous landscape. I hope we can stay here!"

After another uncomfortably long moment of silence, Lonesome George looked over at Dodo and then at the humans. He crawled forward to the edge of the gate and suggested with a calm voice, "I have an idea that is different than your coming in here and as you asked, 'starting over again.' I am one of the newer ones to become extinct and arrive here. However, I think I can speak for all of us since I recently have lived and then died as a result of decades of human interference and neglect for me and my species.

"I became extinct primarily because human intrusions into my original habitat destroyed all of my species except for me. Although late in my life some humans tried to prevent my extinction, I never again had a female to mate with or even a friend of my species for company.

As a result, I have many reasons to be unforgiving when it comes to humans. But I care about all the other creatures I left behind and I want to see them thrive instead of also becoming extinct. I think there is a better option than the two of you coming into Our Forever Home and trying to 'start over.'

"Running away or hiding in a place like Our Forever Home is not the most effective thing you can do to change the course of environmental deterioration," he continued slowly. "It really is not realistic to think somehow you can start everything over again and do it better when you return after living here. While you're here, the world will get even worse than it is right now and may not even be safe to live in when you are ready to return.

"Instead, you should go back to your homes now and take the opportunity to encourage and join with all other humans to work hard immediately to change all the conditions which made Earth more and more uninhabitable. Most of these conditions were created and continue to worsen because of human lifestyles and human failures to care for the planet and environment you all rely on.

"Keep in mind, those conditions include not only those existing just right now but also those which have occurred in past centuries and might occur again in the future. As you probably know, many human scientists and environmentalists believe that a sixth catastrophic extinction event already has started, and only humans can stop it."

Lonesome George hesitated, gathered his thoughts for another moment, and then continued to talk to the two humans. "If you really think about it, the only things that Our Forever Home and its millions of extinct residents can offer you are examples of the consequences of what happens when things go wrong. I already have heard many stories after only one day here about how all animals are unique, how they serve special purposes in the greater environmental scheme, and that they did nothing themselves to deserve becoming extinct.

"There is almost nothing we can do directly from inside Our Forever Home to help save the Earth's animals and plants or help save humans from themselves except for one thing. We can encourage you, and through you other humans, to act more wisely before your race and maybe all other animals and plants become extinct.

"I want to tell you about a wise old African proverb I once heard. It answers the question of who will tell the final story of anyone's future success or failure. The proverb says, 'Until lions have their own historians, tales of the hunt shall always glorify the hunters.' In the future, will you humans tell the story of the future of Earth, or will we?

"Everyone here hopes you will keep that thought in mind when you return home as well as thinking about and acting on what the right course of action is to save yourselves and all the other living creatures on Earth. As much as we would like to help," Lonesome George started to finish, "Your being here for a while won't help you to make the changes that are necessary in behavior, practices, and beliefs to prevent further unnecessary extinctions and to reverse the conditions which threaten the Earth's air, lands, and seas.

"How else can I say this to you more clearly and forcefully? You must be what you want to see! You must not be part of the problem but instead be part of the solution! You must take direct action yourselves, speak truth to power, educate others, and live and act daily as if there is a crisis and each individual person can make a difference.

"We just heard about a single teenage Swedish girl named Greta who had the courage and understanding to challenge powerful politicians and business executives in 2018. She talked to them and tried to impress on them the urgency of immediate corrective action to reverse global warming. She graphically warned them and others like them, 'I want you to act like the house is on fire, because it is!'

"The two of you can and must adopt that motto and join her, her peers, and others with the same concerns and work urgently and diligently to correct the problems created by you and those before you that have led to Earth's current condition. Many American and global organizations actively are trying to make the same changes, but they can't do it alone. They need support and participation from ordinary people like you. Look up the 'New Deal for Nature and People' and join the fight rather than hiding."

When he was through, Lonesome George looked at each one of the humans, trying to see if there were any understanding or acceptance of what he had said. Then he stepped back to the others and looked over to Dodo for her reaction.

"Then what you're both saying…," the man's quiet voice trailed off because he was at a loss for words. "What you're saying…," and his voice trailed off again. "Eve…," he started to say to his companion but couldn't finish that sentence either. She stared at him without saying a word. He then looked back at the animals as if to make one more plea.

Before the two humans could try to argue their point again with the animals in Our Forever Home, Dodo stepped forward to the gate and spoke sharply to end the conversation. She stood up straight, looked directly at them, and advised them, "I am the gatekeeper here. Later, if your sincere efforts to save the world are unsuccessful, we will not hold the failures of your past against the entire human species. Nor will we punish every human for the inability of your renewed efforts to reverse these problems.

"If it becomes necessary because of the extinction of the human race, you can come back to Our Forever Home and we will offer the human race a forever home. But understand, only one of you will be admitted, only the last one of your species."

## *BACKGROUND INFORMATION*

### ***Top Ten Most Endangered Animals: Version A***

1. Pangolin or Spiny Anteater: Is almost hunted to extinction.
2. Rhinos: The Javan Rhino is down to about 60 surviving in a national park and the Sumatran Rhino has less than 100 left in the wild.
3. Sumatran Tiger: About 500 are left, down from over 1,000 in 1978.
4. Vaquita Sea Porpoise: About 10 remained in 2017.
5. Saola or Asian Unicorn: Has only been photographed recently just 3 times.
6. Sumatran Elephant: Less than 2,000 are estimated to still exist.
7. Sumatran Orangutan: 80% of its population is lost, with about 6,600 left.
8. Hawksbill Sea Turtle: 90% of its population is gone from warmer ocean waters.
9. Armur Leopard: Only about 70 are left in the Russian far east.
10. Cross-River Gorillas (200-300 left) and Mountain Gorillas (900 left)

### ***Top Ten Most Endangered Animals: Version B***

From "Ten Most Endangered Animals in the World by 2020" (YouTube) https://www.youtube.com/watch?v=7zqscXFK06U and https://www.youtube.com/watch?v=FsX71DHVO8k

1. Northern White Rhino: Only 2 left.
2. Yangtze Softshell Turtle: Only 3 left.
3. Vaquita: Only 10 left.
4. Northern Sportive Lemur: Only 20 left.
5. South China Tiger: Extinct in the wild, only 24 in zoos.
6. Hainan Baboon: Only 25 left.
7. Asiatic Cheetah: Only 50 left in the wild.
8. Marsican Brown Bear: Only 50 left in the wild.
9. Amu Leopard: Only about 60 left in the wild.
10. Javan Rhino: Only about 67 left.

### ***Organizations Involved in Conservation and Climate Change***

Association of Zoos and Aquariums: Special conservation programs. https://www.aza.org/aza-and-animal-program-conservation-initiatives

Defenders of Wildlife: Protecting and restoring endangered land and marine species in North America and elsewhere. https://defenders.org/

Dian Fossey Gorilla Fund International: Dedicated to the conservation, protection and study of gorillas in their African Habitat. https://gorillafund.org/

Environmental Defense Fund: Uses science, economics, and partnerships to address today's most urgent environmental challenges. https://www.edf.org/

EarthJustice: Uses legal action to protect people's health, protect habitats and wildlife, and combat climate change. https://earthjustice.org/

Friends of the Earth: Exposes those who endanger the health of people and the planet for profit and works to change economic and political rules that create injustice and destroy nature. https://foe.org/

Greenpeace: A global, independent campaigning organization to expose global environmental problems and promote solutions necessary for a green and peaceful future. https://www.greenpeace.org/usa/

Galapagos Conservancy: Dedicated to preserve, protect, and restore the unique biodiversity and ecosystems of the Galapagos Islands. https://www.galapagos.org/

International Rhino Fund: Protects threatened rhinoceros populations in the wild. https://rhinos.org/

Jane Goodall Institute: Promotes understanding and

protection of great apes and their habitat.
https://www.janegoodall.org/

Museums: Check with your local natural history museum for programs about endangered species, dinosaurs, and environmental protection.

Nature Conservancy: Works with people and organizations to protect over 100 million acres of land around the world to preserve wildlife communities.
https://www.nature.org/en-us/

National Resources Defense Council: Uses laws and knowledge to protect wildlife and habitats worldwide, curb global warming, and restore habitats.
https://www.nrdc.org/

National Wildlife Federation: Through habitat protection, restoration, and management, helps bring American endangered species back from the brink of extinction.
https://www.nwf.org/

New Deal for Nature and People. An ambitious global commitment to restore nature.
https://explore.panda.org/newdeal

Ocean Conservancy: Advocates for healthy ocean ecosystems and opposes practices that threaten marine life.
https://oceanconservancy.org/

Panthera: Works to address the dire threats to the world's wild cats. https://www.panthera.org/

PETA (People for Ethical Treatment of Animals): The world's largest animal rights organization. https://www.peta.org/

Photo Ark. Pictorial documentation of thousands of species before they disappear. https://www.joelsartore.com/photo-ark/

Polar Bears International: Works to conserve polar bears and the sea ice they depend on. https://polarbearsinternational.org/

Rainforest Action Network: Takes action against companies and industries driving deforestation and climate change to protect rainforests and enhance environmental justice. www.ran.org

Rainforest Alliance: Conserves biodiversity and ensures sustainable livelihoods by transforming land use, business practices and consumer behavior. https://www.rainforest-alliance.org/

Saving Nature: Works to rescue endangered species from extinction and communities from environmental destruction. https://savingnature.com/

Wildlife Conservation Society: Helps to ensure a future for

Earth's most magnificent creatures and the habitats critical to their survival. https://www.wcs.org/

Wilderness Society: Since 1935, has been protecting wilderness in 44 states and inspiring Americans to care for our wild spaces. https://www.wcs.org/

World Wildlife Fund: Conserves nature and reduces the most pressing threats to the diversity of life on Earth. https://www.worldwildlife.org/

Zoos: Check with your local zoo to see if it participates in the Species Survival Plan Program. https://www.aza.org/species-survival-plan-programs

350. A climate change global grassroots organizing resource seeking a safe climate and better future: "Climate change is about power." https://350.org/

### *Timeline of Earth's Evolution*

EARTH FORMED: (4.54 billion years ago)

ARCHEAN EON: (4.54 billion to 2.5 billion years ago) Earliest single-cell organizations arise in the oceans and also some lived on land.

PROTEROZOIC EON: (2.5 billion to 541 million years ago) Advanced single-cell and multi-cell organisms like sponges appeared. Photosynthesis started.

PHANEROZOIC EON: (541 million years ago to present) It has 3 distinct "eras."

**Paleozoic Era:** ("Ancient Life," 541 million to 250 million years ago It is divided into six "periods.

Cambrian Period (541 million to 485 million years ago) Marine plants and arthropods (animals with an exterior skeleton, segmented body, and jointed legs) like hard-shell creatures called trilobites evolved in the oceans.

Ordovician Period (485 million to 443 million years ago) Early fish, snails, coral, and shellfish joined trilobites; fish with backbones appeared in the oceans; and other arthropods moved onto land where the first plants also appeared. It ended with a mass extinction eliminating 85% of all species

Silurian Period (443 million to 416 million years ago) In the oceans, fish further evolved and developed jaws and bones. On land, early spiders, fungi and centipedes developed.

Devonian Period (416 million to 359 million years ago) Also known as the "Age of Fish" because of their rapid diverse development. Tall plants and trees appeared on land, spiders and four-legged vertebrates evolved on land, and the first amphibians appeared. It ended with a mass extinction event killing 80% of all species

Carboniferous Period (359 million to 299 million years ago) Warmer temperatures on land created swampy-like conditions helped amphibians develop and begin reproduction with eggs. Insects evolved, including flies and dragonflies. Amphibians as big as six feet long and four-legged reptiles continued to develop too.

Permian Period (299 million to 252 million years ago) Larger animals that were the ancestors of cockroaches, dinosaurs, mammals, larger reptiles like crocodiles, turtles and birds appeared. These included large plant-eating and carnivorous. Ninety percent of all insects were 6-legged cockroach-like insects. This period ends with a major extinction event called the "Great Dying" in which 90% of marine species and 70% of land species become extinct.

**Mesozoic Era** ("Middle Life," 252 million to 66 million years ago) It has three distinct periods.

Triassic Period (252 million to 201 million years ago) The Early Triassic was desert-like and saw the revival of smaller reptiles, amphibians, and water animals. The Middle Triassic saw the recovery and growth of small and large water animals, and of larger reptiles, early dinosaurs and small mammal-like animals. The Late Triassic saw continued development of larger dinosaurs such as the flying pterosaurs and a mass extinction event eliminating about 50% of all species.

Jurassic Period (201 million to 145 million years ago) The Early Jurassic was when dinosaurs really began to flourish and rule the land, and around them the first crocodiles and small mammals appeared. The Middle Jurassic was the peak of dinosaur development and competition. During the Late Jurassic, the first bird-like animals such as Archaeopteryx appeared as well as the Stegosaurus and Allosaurus.

Cretaceous Period (145 million to 66 million years ago) During the Early Cretaceous, some dinosaurs disappeared but they were replaced by others. Pterosaurs got bigger and larger mammals including wolf-like predators developed. During the Late Cretaceous, dinosaurs such as the Tyrannosaurus Rex and Triceratops arose and flourished as well as more mammals. This era and period ended with the massive extinction of 75%of all life due to the giant meteorite strike in Mexico and its effects.

**Cenozoic Era** ("New Life," 66 million years ago to present) It also is called "The Age of Mammals" and after the prior extinction event killed almost all dinosaurs, mammals rebounded filling empty niches in global ecosystems. It has three primary divisions and seven lesser ones.

Paleogene Period (formerly called "Tertiary Period) (66 million years to 23 million years ago) It has 3 epochs.

1. *Paleocene Epoch* (66 million years to 56 million years ago) Modern small mammals originated during this time on land dominated by dense forests and sharks ruled the oceans.

2. *Eocene Epoch* (56 million years to 34 million years ago) Larger mammals developed including primates, whales, and horses as forests were replaced by more open areas and grasses.

3. *Oligocene Epoch* (34 million years to 23 million years ago) Animals similar to those today such as cats, dogs, marsupials and elephants evolved.

<u>Neogene Period</u> (23 million years to 2.6 million years ago). It has two epochs.

1. *Miocene Epoch* (23 million years to 5.3 million years ago) Hoofed animals like zebras, apes, and other more modern animals evolved and thrived.

2. *Pliocene Epoch* (5.3 million years to 2.58 million years ago) The earliest man-like animal, Australopithecus, evolved.

<u>Quaternary Period</u> (2.58 million years ago to the present) It has two epochs.

1. *Pleistocene Epoch* (2.58 million to 11,700 years ago). This epoch had 11 ice ages and was the time of large land mammals and reptiles like the Mammoths, Mastodons, Elephant Bids, and Saber Tooth Tigers. Modern humans began to evolve, and Neanderthals became extinct. This Epoch is divided into three somewhat overlapping "Ages" depending on geographic location:

    a. Paleolithic Age, also known as the "Old Stone Age" (2.58 million to 12,000 years ago) The period when humans and pre-humans began to use stone tools.
    b. Mesolithic Age (15,000 to 5,000 years ago) Characterized by the decline in group hunting, the growth of hunter-gatherer lifestyle, and creation of more complex tools.
    c. Neolithic Age, also known as the "New Stone Age" (12,000 to 6,500 years ago) Characterized by the beginning of farming, first use of metal implements and formal communities.

2. *Holocene Epoch* (11,700 years ago to present) This epoch covers the full written history of modern humans and sometimes is called the "Anthropocene Epoch" because its focus is on human activity. It begins with the Bronze and Iron Ages, includes the development of new weapons like bows and arrows, and continues up to the present. During this period, in just 250 years since the Industrial Revolution in the 1800's, the number of animal extinctions has greatly increased again, this time mostly due to human activity.

### *Detailed Human Evolution Interactive Timeline*

See how the various types of humans evolved from apes to ape-like creatures to early humans and then modern humans, presented by the Smithsonian National Museum of Natural History: https://www.aza.org/aza-and-animal-program-conservation-initiatives

### *Downward and Upward World Temperature Trends*

See how temperatures dropped and rose from the beginning of the Paleogene Period to the present with the enormous increases starting 12 million years ago when humans and their ancestors appeared.
https://scitechdaily.com/66-million-years-of-earths-

climate-history-uncovered-puts-current-changes-in-context/

***Mixing Music and Science: "Three Seconds" Explains the Need for Environmental Action in Rap:***

#Film4Climate 1st Prize Short Film Winner - "Three Seconds" on Vimeo. See more at Connect4Climate

***Earth's Climate is Warming: Information and Answers:***

See "NASA Global Climate Change: Vital Signs of the Planet"

***December 2020 United Nations Secretary-General Speech:***

https://www.un.org/sg/en/content/sg/statement/2020-12-02/scretary-generals-address-columbia-university-the -state-of-the-planet-scroll-down-for-language-versions

***A Science Board Game for Young and Old: "Evolve or Perish":***

Play survival through 600 million years in a special Smithsonian Board Game: https://naturalhistory2.si.edu/ETE/ETE_Education&Outreach.Game.html

Made in the USA
Las Vegas, NV
26 January 2021

16559679R10134